The Jerry McNeal Series

Dearly Departed

(A Paranormal Snapshot)

By Sherry A. Burton

 Dorry Press

Also by Sherry A. Burton

The Orphan Train Saga
Discovery (book one)
Shameless (book two)
Treachery (book three)
Guardian (book four)
Loyal (book five)
Patience (book six)
Endurance (book seven)

Orphan Train Extras
Ezra's Story

Jerry McNeal Series (Also in Audio)
Always Faithful (book one)
Ghostly Guidance (book two)
Rambling Spirit (book three)
Chosen Path (book four)
Port Hope (book five)
Cold Case (book six)
Wicked Winds (book seven)
Mystic Angel (book eight)
Uncanny Coincidence (book nine)
Chesapeake Chaos (book ten)
Village Shenanigans (book eleven)
Special Delivery (book twelve)
Spirit of Deadwood (a full-length Jerry McNeal novel, book thirteen)
Star Treatment (book fourteen)
Merry Me (book fifteen)
Hidden Treasures (book sixteen)
Company Business (book seventeen)
Dearly Departed (book eighteen)

***Clean and Cozy Jerry McNeal Series Collection
(Compilations of the standalone Jerry McNeal series)***
*The Jerry McNeal Clean and Cozy Edition Volume one
(books 1-3)*
*The Jerry McNeal Clean and Cozy Edition Volume two
(books 4-6)*
*The Jerry McNeal Clean and Cozy Edition Volume three
(books 7-9)*
*The Jerry McNeal Clean and Cozy Edition Volume four
(books 10-12)*
*The Jerry McNeal Clean and Cozy Edition Volume five
(books 13-15)*
*The Jerry McNeal Clean and Cozy Edition Volume five
(books 16-18)*

***Romance Books** (*not clean* - sex and language)*
Tears of Betrayal
Love in the Bluegrass
Somewhere In My Dreams
The King of My Heart

***Romance Books** (clean)*
Seems Like Yesterday

"Whispers of the Past" (a short story)

Psychological Thrillers
Storm Series
*Surviving the Storm (book one, contains sex, language,
and violence)*
*Sinister Winds (book two, contains language and
violence)*

The Jerry McNeal Series
Dearly Departed

By Sherry A. Burton

A special thanks to

I will forever be grateful to my mom, who insisted the dog stay in the series.

To my hubby, thanks for helping me stay in the writing chair.

To my editor, Beth, for allowing me to keep my voice.

To Laura, for the fantastic covers.

To Amber Legendy, credit for the ship picture on the cover.

To my beta readers for giving the books an early read.

To my proofreader, Latisha Rich, for the extra set of eyes.

To my fans, for the continued support.

Lastly, to my "writing voices," thank you for all the incredible ideas!

Chapter One

The moment Jerry woke, he knew he was alone in the room. That knowledge didn't stop him from running his hand along the bed just to be sure. He blinked to bring the clock into focus—3:29 a.m. While rising early was not unusual for him, April normally preferred to linger under the covers long after waking. Though she professed to love his parents, he wondered if she was tiring of their extended stay at their home in The Villages. Even though she'd stated she was happy staying there, he'd heard it said that a woman likes to have her own kitchen to cook in and wondered if perhaps he should have insisted they rent a place instead of camping out in his parents' spare bedroom. Climbing out of bed, he pulled on his pants and went in search of April.

The house was quiet except for the sound of his bare feet slapping against the cool ceramic tile as he walked. He stopped at Max's room and placed a hand on the door. Not feeling any sign of distress, he focused on April, followed the pull and found her sitting on the couch in the outdoor living area. He started to open the sliding door, then, seeing her eyes closed, debated whether to disturb her.

Gunter lay at her feet staring at the wall that enclosed the space. The dog's ears twitched, letting Jerry know Gunter knew he was there without losing focus on something only the ghostly K-9 could see. That Gunter didn't instantly come to greet him let Jerry know something was amiss. He slid the door open, his gaze scanning the enclosure then focusing on April. A deep frown creased her forehead, and when she looked up, he saw her tear-stained face.

Jerry skirted the table and sat on the couch beside her. "What's wrong?"

She blinked as if just realizing he was there. "I'm a bad mother."

"Is something going on between you and Max?"

"No." The word came out in a sob as she batted fresh tears with the back of her hand.

Jerry started to tell her it was too early in the morning for guessing games, then decided against it. The last thing he wanted was to add to whatever was weighing on her mind. "Tell me what's bothering you, Ladybug, and we'll sort it out together."

"It's Mr. Bigsby." April sniffed.

Jerry recognized the name, as the spirit had been vying for April's attention since first revealing himself to her in DuBois, Pennsylvania. "What's Bigsby have to do with Max?"

"Nothing."

Jerry worked to remain calm. "I can't help you if you don't tell me what's eating at you."

"Mr. Bigsby visited me in my dream, asking for help. Only it wasn't a dream. I mean, it was, but it wasn't. I don't know how to explain it, except that he was able to come to me in my sleep."

Jerry didn't like the idea of strange men invading April's dreams even if the guy was pushing up daisies. *Focus, McNeal.* "What does that have to do with Max?"

"It doesn't."

Jerry rolled his neck.

April rubbed her hands together. "Max used to get these dreams, but she claimed they weren't dreams, and I never believed her."

Okay, now they were getting somewhere. "Not understanding how these things work doesn't make you a bad mother."

"She's my daughter; I should have believed her."

Jerry chuckled. "If I had a nickel for every time my parents didn't believe me, I would be rich."

"Is that supposed to make me feel better?" April snapped.

Apparently not. "I guess not, but I don't think there is a parent alive who doesn't have something they regret. And you must have believed a little of what she told you, or you wouldn't have contacted me. I'm glad you did, by the way. If not, I could still be floating around trying to find something to ground me." Jerry resisted laughing when Gunter groaned.

The groan was replaced by a throaty growl.

Jerry followed the dog's gaze. "Have you spoken to Mr. Bigsby?"

"Not since I woke up. I felt him here, but he still hasn't allowed me to see him."

"He's probably afraid of Gunter," Jerry told her.

"I figured that was why he hasn't spoken. I felt Gunter here and told him to go find you, but I knew he was still here." April heaved a heavy sigh. "How am I supposed to help the spirits if Gunter doesn't let them near me?"

"Gunter is just doing his job."

"No, he's doing what you told him to do." April raised a hand to silence him. "I know you want to protect me, and I love you for that, but that doesn't mean stifling my gift. How is this any different than what your parents did to you when you were a boy?"

The accusation was like a punch in the gut, mainly because it was true. "That wasn't my intention."

"I know. That's why I'm not mad. If I thought you were trying to control me, I wouldn't be here." April reached for his hand. "I'm glad you care enough to be worried about me. I don't know how most of this works, but I'll never figure it out if you don't give me the chance."

Again, there was truth in her words, letting Jerry know he'd been selfish in trying to protect her. "You're right. From now on, there'll be no more handcuffs. You can talk to whomever you want whenever you want, under one condition."

April raised an eyebrow. "Which is?"

"If you feel the slightest bit uncomfortable, you'll call for Gunter. All you have to do is think of him and ask for help and he will show up."

"That's where I have trouble," April confided.

"It's okay to ask for help," Jerry reminded her.

"I know. But I don't like calling for Gunter. What ifhe's busy helping you or Max and I call him for something trivial? I'd never forgive myself if I took him away from either of you."

"Feeling uncomfortable around a spirit isn't trivial."

"No, but what if I pull Gunter away for something that's not as important?"

Jerry smiled recalling a previous conversation with Granny. "You're right. Don't ask for the dogs; just ask for help. Someone will show up."

The brow lifted once again. "Someone?"

"You're one of us now. If you need help, simply ask, and one of the spirits will show up to help you."

"Are you sure?"

Nope. It worked for him, but he was the one who'd been in contact with the spirits in the first place. Would the same hold true if April were to ask? Still, the spirits knew April was part of the family and helping her meant helping him. "Yes, I'm sure." As the words came out of his mouth, he found himself even more determined to see that April had her own dog dedicated to guarding her. He made a mental note to check in with Sinclair to see if Maggie was expecting a litter.

As if reading his mind, Gunter howled a ghostly howl.

"What's wrong with Gunter?" April asked.

"I think he's letting you know he'll do his part to see that you are protected."

"Atta boy, Gunter. I feel better knowing you've got my back."

Not having the heart to tell her what Gunter was really howling about, Jerry let it go. Instead, he spoke to the unseen spirit. "Show yourself, Bigsby."

April sucked in her breath. "You mean he's here? You can see him?"

Jerry shook his head. "I haven't seen him, but I can feel him. My guess is he's been here all along as Gunter hasn't taken his eyes off the area to the right of the pool."

"It's not fair that I can hear spirits but still can't see them."

"I believe you will be able to do both once you hone your abilities." It was another guess, but one he felt confident in giving.

"Do you really think so?"

Before Jerry could answer, Bigsby materialized. Balding and wearing the same dark suit, the man ignored Gunter's growls as he moved closer to the couch and looked at April with hopeful eyes. "You promised to help me." Though the spirit was addressing April, her bewildered stare showed she couldn't see him.

Not wanting her to be at a disadvantage, Jerry pushed off from the couch and pointed to where the spirit stood.

She smiled and adjusted her gaze accordingly so that when she spoke, she looked directly at him. "What can I do for you, Mr. Bigsby?"

"We've been through this before, and you've done nothing. I want you to talk to my wife and let her know the man she is seeing is only after her inheritance money."

As if anticipating this conversation, April pulled a small notebook from her pocket, which she then opened to a page and proceeded to use as a guide to question the man. "How do you know the man is only after your wife's money?"

"Because he first made contact with her shortly after my death."

"Maybe she knew him before, and he was waiting for an opportunity," April offered.

"She didn't know him!" Bigsby snapped.

Before Jerry could counsel the spirit on reeling in his attitude, Gunter growled, and Bigsby eased his tone. "The man clips obituaries. I've seen them."

"I've read about this sort of thing," Jerry said, nodding his head. "Con artists prey on the bereaved by sending out feelers. Once they get a fish on the line, they reel them in."

"That's precisely what he did. He's up to something, I tell you. I've seen him snooping around her desk whenever she leaves the room."

April frowned. "You're a spirit. Can't you scare him away?"

Bigsby laughed a haunting laugh. "I believe

you've watched too much television."

"Can't he do anything to scare the man away?" April asked once more.

Jerry realized April had directed the question at him. "Not if the man can't see or hear him."

"How will he scam her out of her money?"

"He's planning to ask her to marry him" Bigsby said before Jerry could answer. "On the cruise that she paid for."

"Surely she knows he doesn't have any money if he convinced her to pay for the cruise," April suggested.

Bigsby's energy flickered. "She paid because he told her he would reimburse her. Now, he keeps making excuses. He's planning on asking *my* wife to marry him."

"Or, perhaps you're reading things all wrong, and your wife actually does enjoy the man's company," Jerry said, hearing the emphasis on the word "my."

Bigsby kicked a nearby chair and actually managed to scoot it a few inches.

April's face paled as Gunter growled a K-9 warning. "Mr. Bigsby," she said, using her no-nonsense mom tone, "if you can't remain calm, we will not be continuing this conversation."

Atta girl, Ladybug, Jerry thought, beaming his approval.

"I'm sorry," Bigsby said, "but I know what I know, and what I know is the man went to a pawn shop and bought a used ring. It's not even a real diamond but one of those good-looking cubic zirc ones."

"You mean cubic zirconia?" April corrected.

"Whatever. The point is, the thing looks real. It would've fooled me if I hadn't seen him buy it. Made a big show of saying how he was buying it for his fiancée. The pawnshop owner even asked if he shouldn't be buying her a real diamond. The goof said he wouldn't be married to her long enough to warrant a real diamond. Before you go saying anything about her age, my wife was twenty-two years younger than me and is still quite a looker."

"That's young to be a widow," April said softly.

"Tell me about it," Bigsby groaned. "And for the second time, no less."

Something felt off. "How old were you when you died?" Jerry asked.

"Sixty-two."

"I'm assuming you didn't die of natural causes."

Bigsby thumped his chest. "Heart attack. I was heading home to…and so I took one of those little pills. Next thing I knew, I was having a heart attack. I guess that's what I get for marrying a woman twenty-two years younger."

"What about your wife's first husband?"

"Drowned, and before you ask, Lorna wasn't there when it happened. Poor thing's had a bad run of luck, and I aim to see it doesn't continue." Bigsby started pacing the courtyard. "Listen, I'm not so dense that I don't think she'll remarry, but not this guy. Let her find someone who deserves a woman of her talents."

April cocked an eyebrow. "A woman of her talents?"

Bigsby cleared his throat. "My Lorna was a woman with high energy."

Jerry held up his hand when April opened her mouth to ask another question. "I think Mr. Bigsby is saying his wife enjoyed intimacy."

"That she did." Bigsby heaved a long sigh. "What I wouldn't give to…"

"We get the point," Jerry said, cutting him off.

"How long ago did you die, Mr. Bigsby?"

"Going on a year now," Bigsby replied.

"It hasn't been that long. Perhaps Lorna doesn't intend to marry the man. Maybe she just sees this as a way of just having a little…intimacy."

"Nope." The word came without hesitation.

April frowned. "But you said she enjoyed…"

"She did, but that doesn't mean Lorna was a loose woman. Why, she wouldn't even let me…you know, before we were properly married. She said it was the same for her first husband."

The hairs on the back of Jerry's neck were tingling, telling him there was more to this. Given Bigsby's energy was pulsing, he decided to let it go for now. "April and I will see what we can do to help, but it's not going to happen today."

"You'll stop her from marrying the bum?"

"We'll do our best to defuse the situation," Jerry told him. "For now, you'd better go check in with Lorna to see how she's doing."

"Yes, I guess that is a good idea," Bigsby said then disappeared.

"Is he gone?" April asked when Jerry sat beside her once more.

"Yep."

"You think there's more to Lorna than meets the eye, don't you, Jerry?"

"Yep," Jerry said, pivoting toward her. "According to Bigsby, Lorna is a wildcat. I find it hard to believe that a woman who's already done the deed is going to marry a man who's twenty plus years her senior before making sure he can keep up with her needs."

"What about love?"

Jerry shook his head. "We need to work on your detective skills, Ladybug."

"How's that?"

"Because, in all the time Bigsby was talking about his relationship with his wife, he never once used the word love."

Chapter Two

Though Jerry had convinced April to return to bed with him, she was gone again by the time he woke. He found her sitting at the dining room table, so caught up with something on her computer screen that she never looked up when he entered.

Gunter, on the other hand, got up and happily trotted to Jerry's side, positioning himself under Jerry's hand. Jerry scratched the dog behind the ears for several moments before speaking. "I thought you were going to try and get some sleep."

April jumped and splayed a hand across her chest as if trying to calm her heartbeat. "You scared the crap out of me."

This wasn't a *you startled me* response. This was a *you caught me doing something I shouldn't be doing* response. He noted her credit card lying on the table next to the computer and instantly knew what she'd been up to. "You know I can get that done for free. Heck, you know how to get into the computer in the Durango. You could have done it that way," Jerry said with a nod to April's laptop.

April sat back in the chair and crossed her arms. Her messy hair, which floated aimlessly around her face, and the puffy circles beneath her eyes let him know she hadn't slept.

"When am I going to get those kinds of psychic powers?" Her voice was hopeful.

He chuckled. "That wasn't being a psychic. That was knowing you like I do."

"Okay, Mr. Wise Guy, you tell me what I've been doing." Her smirky smile belied her tone.

Jerry leaned back against the counter and crossed his feet. Gunter took his presence as a release from guard duty. He lowered to the tile and rolled onto his back, wiggling from side to side as if scratching an invisible itch.

"My guess…" Jerry watched as Gunter stood then moved to a stream of sunlight before lowering once more and closing his eyes as he flopped to his left side. "You climbed out of bed the moment you knew I was asleep and have been searching social media for Lorna hoping to find clues to prove she killed both of her husbands. Having found her but not gathering the evidence you wanted, you then paid to get her personal records so you could continue your search. That about sum things up?"

April blew the hair from her face. "Maybe."

"You know, one phone call, and I can…" Jerry began.

"What would be the fun of that?" April pouted.

"Besides, Mr. Bigsby came to me. Shouldn't I be the one to solve this?"

"If it was a simple case of telling the woman not to marry the man, yes, but we both know there's more to this than that." Jerry nodded toward the computer. "Find anything interesting?"

April's smirk spread into a wide grin. "She's guilty!"

Jerry raised an eyebrow. "You found proof?"

"Not concrete, but her page is only a few years old."

Jerry laughed.

"No, I'm serious. The account was created about the same time she would have met her husband—Bigsby," April said before he asked. "From the moment she created it, everything she posted was a perfect diary of how they met, what they did together, and how much in love they were. Then radio silence for a couple of days around the time he died, followed by 'woe is me' posts right up until the time Bigsby said she met this new guy."

"I hate to tell you this, Ladybug, but you've just described most social media accounts. How does any of that prove the woman's guilty of committing murder?"

"It didn't, until I did a background search and googled her under her previous address and found she had another account under her previous married name. The posts are almost identical leading up to her first husband's death. Her friends even offered to send money to help with her expenses."

"Bigsby said she'd inherited a lot of money."

"Exactly! But that didn't stop her from thanking them and telling them she would inbox them with the details. And get this, none of her previous friends show up as mutual friends on her Bigsby account." April blew at the strand of hair once more. "I can see losing some friends, but I'm telling you, I can't find one single friend that followed her from one page to the next."

"That is odd," Jerry agreed. "Let me guess, her first husband died of a heart attack."

April bobbed her head. "In the swimming pool at the Y. Lots of witnesses, but Lorna wasn't one of them."

"Which means no one would have suspected her of killing the guy," Jerry said, reading her mind.

"She even made a post giving details of the day and how normally she would have been there with him, and how she could have saved him if she herself hadn't stayed home that day."

"Sounds like she did a good job covering her tracks," Jerry mused.

"Too good."

"How's that?"

"No evidence. According to the obituaries, both men were cremated. And since the men didn't have families and none of her friends knew of her previous husband, there was no one around to question the fact she'd lost two husbands within such a short period of time."

"How do you know none of her friends knew?"

"Because, while the woman is good, she doesn't seem to know enough to lock down her social media accounts so people like me can't stalk their accounts. A part of me wonders if she left everything visible on purpose to appear normal. Most people wouldn't think to question how new the account is, and if one of her new friends does ask, she can throw them off by claiming she'd been hacked and had to start a new account."

"You said the gap between marriages was short. How short?" Jerry asked.

"She married Bigsby fourteen months after losing her first husband. She was married to each just under two years before they died. Each time, she had a seven-month courtship before moving out of state and tying the knot. She hasn't posted anything to her account since shortly after Bigsby died, but according to him, she's been seeing this guy for seven months."

"So, if she is planning on doing this again, then this new fellow fits within the timeline."

"Exactly!" April said confidently. "It's a pattern. I'm sure she has a new social media account that I haven't found yet."

"You said she moves, which makes sense if she doesn't want to get caught, but where do these friends come from?"

"She's pretty and single. It's not hard to make friends," April told him. "I just don't understand her motivation."

Jerry raised an eyebrow. "For killing her

husband? I'm going with money."

"But why go through all the trouble of making friends and blasting her life on social media? Wouldn't it be better to just stay under the radar?"

"The woman is either very smart or incredibly dense," Jerry agreed. "I think it's quite brilliant, actually."

April blinked her surprise. "Really?"

"Sure, how many people do you know without a social media account?"

"So you're saying she's doing this to appear normal?"

"I'm not a shrink, but that'd be my guess. Let me ask you this: you've spent hours scouring through her accounts; if not for your conversation with Bigsby, would anything you saw raise any red flags?"

April shook her head. "No, if I didn't suspect anything, it would all seem normal. Both accounts show a happy bride followed by a grieving widow."

Jerry looked when Gunter lifted his head and woofed his agreement.

April's smile faded. "What's Gunter barking at?"

"Gunter's good," Jerry assured her. "He's just agreeing with you."

April giggled and pointed to the hallway. "Or, he knows your parents are awake."

Jerry matched her smile. "That was my next guess."

Another giggle. "Good one, Mr. Psychic."

Gunter scrambled to his feet as Wayne and Lori

entered the room. "You two are up early," Lori said, heading to the coffee pot with Gunter on her heels.

"We're working a case," April told her.

Jerry shook his head. "Not true, April is close to solving this one all on her own."

Lori peered at April over her cup. "Atta girl, April."

April beamed under the compliment, then switched her gaze to Max, who'd just entered with Houdini at her side. "Good morning, Maxine. Did you sleep well?"

Max shrugged. "I guess."

Lori poured a glass of fresh orange juice and set it on the counter. "Here, sweetie, this will turn that frown upside down"

Max grinned. "Thanks, Grandma."

"There, you see. It worked already." Lori winked.

"Would this be a ghost case or a human case?" Wayne asked.

"Spirits are human," Max said, lowering her glass. "They're just dead."

Wayne shook his head as he took hold of a cup of coffee Lori offered. "They can't be human if they're dead."

"Why not? They still have bodies," Max countered. "I've seen them."

Wayne looked over the rim of the cup. "Ghosts have bodies?"

"Sure, we couldn't see them if they didn't. Isn't that right, Jerry?" Max said.

"Technically, they are just borrowing the image of the body they used to inhabit," Jerry mused.

"What happens if their body isn't here?" Lori asked. "Say, for instance, someone gets cremated."

"They still show up using the body they had," Max answered. "Mr. Bigsby was cremated, and he still shows up as he was."

"The good Lord must give us a pretty long lease on these things." Wayne lowered the cup and looked at his hands. "You'd think they'd come with a better warranty."

"They do," Lori interjected. "We mere mortals just forgot to read the owner's manual somewhere along the way."

"So, what's this big case?" Wayne asked.

"Mr. Bigsby thinks his widow is being scammed and wants April to warn her, but near as we can tell, his widow is no saint," Jerry told him.

Wayne arched an eyebrow. "So you're thinking the scammer is about to get scammed?"

"Or worse." Jerry looked at April. "You fill them in on your brilliant detective work while I go make a phone call."

April raised an eyebrow. "Is the call to Fred or Seltzer?"

Jerry rocked back on his heels. "Why would I bring Seltzer in on this?"

"Because he and June are booked on the same cruise as Mrs. Bigsby and her friend." April shrugged. "I may have stalked June's page as well."

Jerry shook his head. "Ladybug, you missed your

calling. You should have been a detective, and if I hadn't already asked you to marry me, this would clinch the deal."

"You sure got a keeper, that's for sure," his father said, bobbing his head. "Does that mean you two are going on a cruise?"

"If you're going on a cruise, I want to go too!" Max's voice was hopeful.

"I'm afraid none of us are going," April said, tempering the mood. "At least not on that ship. That cruise is sold out. That's why I was thinking you'd call Seltzer, since he's the only one who's going to be able to do anything."

"This would be out of his jurisdiction," Jerry said. "Nope, this is a Fred call. I'll get him to get us on the ship."

"I just told you the cruise is sold out."

Jerry smiled a sly smile. "Oh, ye of little faith."

"I have plenty of faith in my knowledge that there are only so many cabins on the ship, and according to the website, those cabins are sold out. Before you say they can find a room, just remember they only have so many lifeboats."

"She has a point," Wayne agreed.

"I'll get us on that cruise, and there'll be enough lifeboats." Jerry instantly regretted the promise at seeing April's face light up. "Let me make a few phone calls."

"Hey, Jer," Wayne called as he was leaving. "See if you can get me and your ma on that ship too."

So much for a romantic cruise. Jerry stifled a

groan.

"Do you really mean it, Wayne?" Lori's voice was full of excitement.

"Sure," Wayne said, bobbing his head. "If Jerry can get us tickets."

"I'll see what I can do, Pop." It was said more by reflex than actually meaning it, but as he left the room, Jerry thought maybe having his parents along on the cruise wouldn't be a bad thing, as he knew they'd be thrilled to watch over Max while he and April enjoyed some alone time. Even as the thought came to him, Jerry realized it wouldn't be as simple as having Fred conjure up five tickets. They were going to need three cabins, and with all the talk about lifeboats, the cabins would have to be in the same area. Neither he nor April would dream of getting into a lifeboat without making sure Max, his parents, and Houdini were safely on board. Gunter was a nonissue since the ghostly K-9 could come and go at his leisure. If push came to shove, he knew the same was true with Houdini, not that he worried about the ship sinking with them on board, as he felt more than certain both his and Max's spidey senses would give them ample warning if something were to go awry.

As he pulled out his phone, another thought occurred to him: if he could convince April to tie the knot on the ship, it would take away the pressure of having a huge ceremony. With Seltzer, June, and his parents on board, they would be surrounded by those who mattered most. An image of Carrie flashed in his mind, followed by images of Fred and Barney. One by one, those he'd come to think of as family also flittered into focus. Okay, not so perfect after all, but no different than running to the courthouse as April had suggested on more than one occasion.

Chapter Three

"McNeal, what can I do for you on this fine morning?" Fred asked.

"I need a miracle," Jerry said, cutting to the chase.

"Are we talking about a small miracle or an over-the-top circus performance kind of thing?" Fred asked, playing along.

"A Fred miracle," Jerry informed him. "I need three rooms on a fully booked cruise ship that leaves in three days."

To his credit, Jefferies neither laughed nor disconnected the call. "Anything else?"

"The rooms need to be close together in case the ship sinks." Once again, Jerry could picture the man on the other end of the call rocking back on his heels as if he thought he was being punked.

"Is that a possibility?"

"Is what a possibility?"

"The ship sinking." Fred's voice was devoid of humor.

"Not on my end, but April has seen the *Titanic* movie one too many times." Jerry paced the room, stepping over Gunter, who lay stretched out across the bedroom floor. Reaching the far wall, he turned and retraced his path. While the dog's gaze followed, he never bothered to move out of the way; then again, that was the way with spirits.

"What's the name of the ship? And why do you need to be on this particular cruise?" Fred asked.

"The *Duchess of the Sea*."

"You want to take a vacation with your former boss," Fred said before Jerry could say anything else.

That Fred knew Seltzer's schedule didn't come as a surprise—Fred Jefferies knew everything. "Brian and his wife will be on the cruise, but this has nothing to do with him unless you can't get us on board, and then we might want to use him as a backup plan. Me and April getting on the ship is work-related, but now Max and my folks want to come."

"Your former boss, his wife, your parents, Max, and the two of you. Sounds like the makings of a wedding party," Fred said.

Okay, that part was a little creepy, as the idea had occurred to him as well. "I wouldn't be opposed to that if the opportunity were to present itself."

"No can do," Fred said firmly.

"You're saying I can't marry April?"

"Oh, you can marry the girl; you just can't do it on that cruise ship. Not anytime soon, anyway.

They're totally booked."

"That was the reason for the Fred-sized miracle. It's work-related—trouble with a spirit."

"Listen, I could probably get you on board as a member of the crew, but asking for a room is doubtful; requesting three rooms, even in different areas, is out of the question. You go, fix whatever needs fixing, and then we'll set the wedding party up on their own charter when all is said and done. How does that sound?"

Terrific, actually, but it wouldn't solve the current dilemma. "I can't fix this one on my own." Jerry started to fill Fred in on the details when his boss cut him off.

"Passing Max off as one of the crew is going to be a bit tricky."

"I don't need Max. I need April. The spirit will only talk to her." It was the last thing he'd wanted to say, as he knew the implications, and even though he knew Fred would have eventually found out, he'd hoped to keep April's ability on the down-low just a bit longer to give her time to adapt. Jerry gave his words a moment to sink in before continuing. "April can hear spirits. It started while we were in Pennsylvania, and she's been working with them for a few weeks. There is one spirit, a fellow by the name of Bigsby, who is relentless in reaching out to her. The guy thinks someone is out to scam his wife and, for some reason, thinks April is the only one who can help him. Only he didn't count on April being so tenacious. She has a pretty strong feeling that the wife murdered both Bigsby and her previous husband, only we can't prove it because both men were cremated."

"This Bigsby fellow can't corroborate her hunch?" Fred asked, ignoring the new revelation.

"He's in denial. Anyway, both the wife and her new victim slash scammer will be on the cruise, and we thought we could figure out a way to catch both of them."

"Have you stopped to think that the reason the spirit chose April is that she is so tenacious?"

"Meaning?"

"I won't presume to even begin to know how this all works, but what if that's why he chose her? Anyone else might have worked to expose the scammer, but deep down, he knows what happened to him, and figures April would be diligent enough to root around until she had uncovered the big picture."

The theory had legs. "Not bad," Jerry replied.

"I have my moments. Listen, I can't make any promises, but I'll see what I can do. In the interim, if the spirit won't talk to you, then you might want to consider forming a backup plan."

"I'm already working on it."

"I know you're not going to suggest April go on that cruise alone."

"Nope, she doesn't have the experience. But we have someone who does."

"Seltzer can talk to spirits?"

"No, but he wouldn't need to as we already know

the key players and have an inkling of their agendas."

"Get him up to speed, and we'll work out the details. Got to go; I have a miracle to perform. Oh, and McNeal?"

"Yeah, boss?"

"Tell April I said welcome to the team. I'll send over a contract for her to sign as soon as it's written up."

"She's still honing her abilities," Jerry said before realizing Fred had already disconnected the call. Before he was able to make his next call, the hair on the back of his neck crawled, letting him know he wasn't alone. A second later, his grandmother appeared.

Wearing a sheer coverup over a conservative one-piece bathing suit, Betty Lou looked as beach-worthy as anyone else living in The Villages except for the fact she'd been dead for a number of years. Luckily for them, spirits could manifest in any form, and she looked younger and firmer than previous visits.

"Why so glum, Jerry? You knew it was only a matter of time before Fred found out what April could do." That she'd listened in on his and Fred's conversation didn't come as a surprise.

"I know. It's not that. I knew the implications the moment I said it."

"Then what's bothering you?" Granny asked.

"If we don't get this Bigsby thing sorted out, he's going to continue to haunt April. I don't want that hanging over our heads when we finally say our vows, not that I expect that to happen any time soon as, normally, Fred would say consider it done. Today, he said he'd see what he could do."

"Oh boo." She smiled as if laughing at her own joke. "When has that man ever let you down?"

Granny had a point. Fred was a mover and a shaker. If anyone could get them on the ship, it was him. "I guess I should tell April in case she needs to do some shopping."

"Of course she'll need to shop, but that can wait a bit." Granny sat and patted the bed. "Sit with me for a moment."

"Problem?" Jerry asked, lowering to the bed. That Granny had been absent of late wasn't lost on him. He'd also wondered about Bunny's absence but decided not to ask, fearing the mere mention of the eccentric spirit would cause her to materialize.

"No, I just wanted to ask how Max is doing."

"Max is fine. Wait, is there something going on that I don't know?"

"No. Nothing new anyway; she's a kid, and kids hold grudges. She's still mad at me and Bunny because of what happened in Pennsylvania," Granny told him.

"Are you sure? She hasn't mentioned it."

"She's thirteen, and in her mind, we almost destroyed her family. It doesn't matter that it isn't true, but she's a child, and children don't always see the big picture."

They hadn't really spoken about what happened

since he'd had his epiphany in the jail cell. Jerry got the feeling Granny was ready to revisit the matter. "You're saying there's more to the story than teaching me a lesson?"

"There's always more to the story. Do you know why we chose that particular boy?" Granny asked.

"Because he was deaf?"

"Because it wasn't the first time he'd run into the street. He'd done so numerous times, even before they got the dog. Running after a ball. Chasing after a butterfly. He once ran out on a dare by the older kids who like to play in their yard."

"His mother didn't know?"

"She knew. But it is always easier to blame others—in this case, the dog—than accept your own negligence."

"Perhaps I should say something."

Granny waved him off. "No need to worry the authorities. She's a good mother; she just needs a push in the right direction. It's been taken care of."

"Dare I ask how?"

"Sure. Bunny put someone on her."

What does that even mean? "You're saying Bunny is having someone possess the woman?"

"Don't be silly; we don't sanction possessions. Bunny assigned someone to help watch over the boy and give the mother a little nudge if need be."

"A guardian angel?"

"Of sorts. This one has a little more spunk than some and should be a good fit to keep the boy safe. Plus, the dog seems to like her, and that's huge."

"Because not all dogs like having spirits hanging around." As the words came out of his mouth, Jerry had an epiphany. Growing up, he never liked dogs because they never seemed to like him. It wasn't him the dogs didn't like; it was the spirits that were often near.

Gunter groaned. Opening his eyes, the dog looked at Jerry as if to say, "Took you long enough to figure that one out."

"I'm sure Max would be open to hearing the rest of the story," Jerry said, ignoring the imagined quip. "Do you want me to call her in so we can discuss it?"

"No, not yet. Let her enjoy her time with Lori."

Jerry smiled his understanding. "I thought jealousy was an earthly emotion."

"I'm not jealous. I'm thrilled that Max enjoys Lori's company. Your mother adores her, and I'm happy they get to spend time together."

Once again, Jerry understood the words left unspoken. While Betty Lou was pleased she'd gotten to know the girl, she wished she'd gotten to do so while still alive. "Max is lucky to have you in her life."

"Only Max?"

Jerry smiled. "We all are—April too."

Gunter gave a soft woof.

"We're happy to have you too, boy," Jerry said, meaning it.

Gunter answered by thumping his tail on the tile floor.

"Listen, while I appreciate all these kumbaya moments, I've got work to do. I need to call Seltzer and get him up to speed in case Fred can't get us on the ship."

"I can take a hint; if you need me, I'll be in the pool." Instead of disappearing, Granny stood and walked straight through the wall.

Jerry moved to the window. Sure enough, both his grandmother and Bunny were floating on rafts in the backyard pool. Each had a glass of brightly colored liquid topped off with an equally bright pink umbrella.

As if feeling him looking, Bunny lifted her sunglasses and offered a pinky wave.

Afraid to encourage her, Jerry backed away from the window and used his phone to call Seltzer.

"Jerry, my boy, what's the good word?" Seltzer's voice was uncharacteristically jovial, causing Jerry to wonder if he, too, was enjoying some refreshments by the pool.

"Sounds like Florida is agreeing with you," Jerry said.

"What can I say? June was right. All work and no play made Brian a dull boy. I just needed a little fun in the sun to get me right again. How about you? Are you calling to tell me you've set a date, or are you calling to bend my ear about the latest fascinating case you're working on?"

"If things go my way, solving one would solve the other." Jerry went on to explain about Bigsby and their suspicions regarding his wife, and how she would soon be departing on the same cruise.

"And you're telling me it is a mere coincidence this ghost's wife and her victim/scammer will be on the same cruise as me and June?"

"I can't see any connection other than plain luck of the draw," Jerry replied. "But I think it's a sign that it's meant to be. Plus, if we do get on the ship and get things settled, we can ask the captain to marry us. I don't know what's involved, but if this all works out, having you and June witness us saying our vows would mean a lot to me. My parents want to come along, so I don't have to worry about them being upset about missing the wedding."

"From what I've heard, the cruise is booked. You think that boss of yours will be able to pull this off ?"

And that was the million-dollar question. "No clue. I'm afraid even Fred Jefferies has his limitations. But I guess if it can be done, Fred's the one to make it happen."

"That Bigsby fellow wants it done bad enough, perhaps he could pull some strings," Seltzer mused.

"I'm not sure spirits can pull strings." It was a lie. Jerry knew all too well what spirits were capable of; he just wasn't prepared to have that conversation. "Which is the real reason for the call. Would you be interested in doing a little undercover work if we can't get on the ship?"

"Undercover work, you say?"

"I know you are enjoying your vacation, and I wouldn't even ask…"

"No need to apologize."

Had Seltzer been at his desk, the man would have flipped backward in his chair. As it was, Jerry could picture him reaching for a stick of gum while mulling it over. To Jerry's knowledge, Seltzer had never done any undercover work, so he decided to give the man an out. "Of course, I know you'll need to talk this over with June since this is supposed to be a vacation."

"June? Yes, of course." Seltzer sounded more disappointed than relieved. "Let me have a chat with her. I'll be in touch later today."

"Sounds good."

Gunter scrambled to his feet the second Jerry ended the call.

Jerry eyed the dog. "Not a word to anyone about the possibility of me and April getting hitched on the cruise ship, and that goes for anyone else who might be listening," he said to the air.

Gunter merely looked at him as if to say, "You know I can't talk, right?"

Jerry clapped his hand to his chest. Gunter jumped at the invitation.

"Ya know, fellow," Jerry confided. "I never pictured myself with a wife, a house, a swell kid, and a mangy old dog, but here I am, living the dream."

Acting every part of a trusted companion, Gunter slobbered the side of Jerry's face with eager canine kisses.

Chapter Four

Max

Max fidgeted in her seat, unable to contain her excitement about the possibility of going on her first cruise. She took out her phone, thinking to text Chloe. The girl was her best friend, but it kind of stung when she bragged about the places she went to with her parents. At least, it used to. Since working for the agency, Max was quickly catching up. Still, to Max's knowledge, Chloe had never been on a cruise, and this would be her chance to brag about getting to go on one.

"Max," April cautioned, "perhaps you should wait to tell Chloe until we are sure Fred can make this happen."

Max peered at her mother. "Are you reading my mind?"

"No, I'm being a mom who knows her daughter. You tell Chloe everything." April closed the laptop before standing and arching her back. "Listen, I know how eager you are to share this with her, but maybe it's better to wait until we know we have something to share."

Max knew her mother had included herself in the "we," as she would be quick to share the news with her own best friend, Carrie. "Okay, Mom, I'll wait."

"You two can wait to tell whoever you want, but if there is a chance we're going on a cruise, I think we should head out in the next hour or so to beat traffic," Lori said.

Max looked at her mother, who seemed just as confused as she was.

"Head out to where?" April asked, mirroring Max's thoughts.

"Why shopping, of course. You two will need cruise attire. Since Max lives in the pool, she will need a few more swimsuits. And you will need some things as well. Your shorts are fine and all, but you'll need a bit more color on the ship. Plus, there's formal night and shoes. You'll need some shoes."

Max slid from the stool, thinking of retrieving the suit she'd left to dry in the courtyard. As she reached the glass doors, she saw Bunny lying on a raft in the pool. Wearing a bright one-piece fuchsia bathing suit and holding a drink that looked equally festive, the spirit must have felt her watching, as she lifted her sunglasses and smiled a fluorescent-lipped smile that faded when Max failed to return her grin. Max showed no emotion as she moved away from the door.

Wayne's protests pulled her back to the moment. "Dagnabbit, woman, I don't need any new clothes.

I've barely worn what's in my closet as it is."

Lori shook her head and sighed as if dealing with a child. "That's because you insist on wearing the same outfits day after day. I barely take that shirt you have on out of the dryer and you're wearing it again."

"What's the matter with wearing it if it's clean?" Wayne huffed.

"The problem is people are going to think that's the only shirt you own."

"Do you think I give a …"

"Wayne!" Lori said, cutting him off. "Watch your language. Max is in the room."

"Oh, phew, the girl's a teenager. I'm sure she's heard it all before," Wayne said then offered Max a wink.

Max giggled.

"Not from her grandfather, she hasn't!" Lori said firmly enough to silence the man.

While Max wanted to confirm Wayne's deductions, she hadn't heard Lori use that tone before and thought she should stay out of their squabble.

Max!

It took a second for Max to realize her mother hadn't spoken her name out loud. She looked to see her mother stealthily pointing toward the hallway where Houdini was standing in the hall with his head poked through the bedroom door. It wouldn't have been so bad, but the bedroom door was closed, and while Jerry's parents knew about Houdini being half-ghost, Jerry had said it would be best if they didn't remind them of it.

Max excused herself in the pretense of getting ready and hurried down the hall. Taking hold of Houdini's hind legs, she attempted to pull him out of the door. Much to her chagrin, her socked feet were no match for the tile floor, and she quickly found herself sitting on the ground with Houdini's tail waving like a flag in her face. She was about to tell him to knock it off when she heard Jerry's voice drift through the door. *"If we do get on the ship and get things settled, we can ask the captain to marry us. I don't know what's involved, but if this all works out, having you and June witness us saying our vows would mean a lot to me. My parents want to come along, so I don't have to worry about them being upset about missing the wedding."*

Max leaned in, hoping to hear more, but she only heard footsteps and knew Jerry was pacing the floor. *He's nervous!* She swallowed, wondering if he was nervous about getting married or about something going wrong and not being able to. He was right, though. While her mother seemed happy about his proposal, she had been putting off planning the actual wedding. She'd heard of people getting cold feet, but she didn't think that was the case with her mom. Max had no doubt her mother loved Jerry, but she also felt perhaps she was just afraid of messing up again. Hoping to hear more, she tugged on Houdini. This time, the dog backed out on his own and began slathering her with kisses.

Max giggled as she pushed him away. Not wanting to be caught eavesdropping, she scooted closer to the door and gave Houdini the signal to lie down. Now, if Jerry were to open the door, she would explain she'd been reprimanding the dog for his actions.

As she leaned closer to the door, Jerry's words floated out once again, *"Ya know, fellow, I never pictured myself with a wife, a house, a swell kid, and a mangy old dog, but here I am, living the dream."*

Max knew he was talking to Gunter, which meant he'd ended the call. Not wanting to be discovered listening, she scrambled to her feet. As she hurried to her room, Jerry's words kept repeating in her mind: he thinks I'm a swell kid. Okay, so it might not be the most poetic thing anyone had ever said about her, but in all her thirteen years, not one of the father figures in her life had said anything even remotely close.

***

Houdini followed her into her bedroom and jumped onto the bed, sniffing at the sketchbook that lay just beside her pillow. Weird, as she distinctly recalled placing it in the drawer of her nightstand. Instantly on guard, Max looked around the room to see if anything else was out of place.

Nothing was.

Nor had she seen anyone venture down the hall. Convincing herself she'd simply forgotten to put it away, she moved Houdini aside and picked up the sketchbook. The instant she touched it, she knew something had been added.

Max closed her eyes, flipping through the book and listening to the pages rustle until her fingers stilled. Opening her eyes once more, she sucked in her breath. There, on the page in front of her, was the little boy they almost hit in Pennsylvania. Houdini whined as her heart drummed in her chest. The memory of the ordeal came flooding back, instantly ruining her good mood. Though sirens from Jerry's SUV had echoed off the side of the mountain, the boy was deaf and unaware of the looming danger as he ran out into the road. Chasing after his dog, he would have met his demise if not for both her and her mother yelling for Jerry to stop…

Max narrowed her eyes, recalling the events leading up to and after that near-tragic incident and how the two spirits she'd trusted most had used her to help teach Jerry a lesson. The sketch was darker than most of the others in her book, showing how angry she had been when sketching the image. She hated the image and all it represented so much that she had almost ripped it out of the book many times.

"Turn the page." Granny's words floated over her shoulder.

Of course Granny had been behind this. Who else? "What? You don't like being reminded of your handiwork?" Max snapped.

"I am all too aware of the events of that day along with what it cost me," Granny said sadly.

Max wanted to remind her that she was the one who'd gotten hurt. She who had to live with the pain of having let Jerry down. "You shouldn't have butted in."

"Max, please turn the page," Granny said once more.

This time, Max listened. Only the image on the page wasn't one she recognized. Not in its entirety anyway. While it was the same little boy and the same street in front of the same house, the scene showed the little boy chasing a monarch butterfly. She turned the page to show the same boy chasing a ball, and another showing him standing in the middle of the road facing a blind curve.

"I don't understand." Max stared at the page, then turned to find others she'd drawn since, leaving no blank pages in between. "I didn't draw these, and there were not any blank pages. How did they get there?"

"The how is not important. It's the why I want you to see. Look at the photos again."

Max thought about the little boy as she flipped back through the images. Suddenly, she was there watching as each image came to life, first with the rambunctious child running after a large orange and black butterfly. Absorbed in the chase, the boy ran around the yard, weaving back and forth as the insect changed its path to avoid capture. As the butterfly set out across the road, the little boy followed. As the winged creature flew out of range, the child altered his course to walk the yellow center line in the middle of the road tightrope fashion, with his arms stretched as if helping retain balance while walking toward the blind curve. The boy's mother ran to pull him from the street, then, after giving him a firm wag of the finger, went back inside the house, leaving him to continue playing in the yard.

Max shuddered as she shook off the image and turned the page, sending another image live. The boy was all smiles and giggles as he kicked a soccer ball around the yard until one errant kick sent the ball skidding across the grass and into the street. Mindless of the danger, the boy ran to collect it. A car flashed in her mind's eye, and the boy was no more.

Her eyes widened with the knowledge of what could have been. "The mother just left him."

"That's because she had another child inside. A baby she'd left unattended that she had to check on."

"You didn't use the boy. You sent Jerry to save him."

"It was only a matter of time until something happened to him. We knew we could control the outcome and, in turn, not only help Jerry see what his denouncement of our help had brought, but also get the mother the help she needed to keep the boy safe." Granny's smile faded. "Bunny and I thought it was a win for everyone. We didn't count on you being so upset with us."

"Why didn't you tell me? I've been so mad at you."

"I guess we thought you just needed a bit of time to get over it."

Max cocked an eyebrow. "I'm a kid. Kids don't

get over things. They dwell on them, and that makes things worse. Seriously, I wasn't sure I ever wanted to see you again."

Houdini moved between them as if to prove the point.

Granny's energy faded.

"No, don't go. I'm better now that you explained things. I've missed you." Max smiled when Granny's energy brightened.

Houdini yipped. A second later, there was a knock on the door. Max knew it was Jerry even before she invited him in.

Jerry frowned. "Everything okay in here?"

"We're good," Max said, bobbing her head. "Granny is just explaining some things."

A smile replaced the frown. "Step into the living room for a moment so I can update you all at the same time."

"Okay, Jerry, I'll just be another moment." Max waited for Jerry to close the door. "We're going shopping because Uncle Fred is trying to get us on a cruise."

"Lucky you. I always wanted to go on a cruise but never crossed it off my bucket list."

"I'm not sure we are going either. Uncle Fred might not be able to get us rooms. Jerry doesn't know I know, but if we get on the cruise, he plans on asking the captain to marry him and Mom."

"I'm glad my Jerry has finally found someone to ground him," Granny replied.

"I was thinking," Max's voice was hopeful, "that

maybe you could help Uncle Fred get us on the ship."

"What was that you said earlier about my not butting in?"

"That was before I knew the truth. I'm sorry I didn't trust you."

"No, child, it is I who should apologize. I should have made things clearer from the beginning."

"So, you'll help?"

Bunny appeared next to Granny. "We'd be delighted to."

"Now, Bunny, don't go getting the child's hopes up," Granny told her.

"Oh pooh, don't go being a spoilsport," Bunny said, waving her off. "We've just gotten back into the girl's good graces; we can't let her down now."

"How do you suppose we fix it?" Granny asked.

"I used to be a travel agent," Bunny said. "Wow, I'd completely forgotten that one until now."

"I'm sure it was a great job, but it won't help us now," Granny told her. "The ship is full, and they're going to need multiple rooms."

Bunny was undeterred. "Then we have to get creative."

"It better be something good, because the only way we can pull this off is to cancel the wedding."

"Not bad," Bunny surmised. "We can give the bride cold feet."

While Max wanted to get on the ship so her mom and Jerry could get married, it didn't seem right to do so at another woman's expense. "No, it's not fair to not let them get married."

"What if we just have them postpone it for a bit?" Granny asked. "Would you be okay with that?"

"They'd still get married?"

"We'll arrange it ourselves and make sure it's even better than they'd hoped."

"Okay," Max agreed.

"Sushi!" Bunny exclaimed.

Max wrinkled her nose. "You're saying I have to eat raw fish?"

Bunny leaned in, whispering a conspiratorial whisper. "Not you, my dear, the wedding party!"

"That would work," Granny agreed.

"Care to fill me in?" Max's request was met with silence as both spirits disappeared.

Chapter Five

Jerry scanned the living area, saw Max was missing, and held up a finger, letting the others know he'd be a moment, and continued on to her room. He hated hearing there were ill feelings between his grandmother and Max, especially since his actions had been instrumental in causing the disconnect. It didn't help that he'd failed to realize there was a problem in the first place. If he was going to step into the dad role, he would need to pay closer attention to such things. As such, he wanted to ensure Max was giving Granny a chance to explain herself and offer to work as a go-between if that weren't the case.

The moment she invited him into her room, the energy let him know he'd been worried for nothing; Max's smile cemented that thought. He let her know she was needed in the other room, then stepped back into the hall to wait for her.

"I take it you two were able to work things out," he said when she opened the door.

"Yep, we're cool."

"I didn't know there was a problem," Jerry said, tipping his hand.

Max shrugged. "I didn't want to trouble you."

Jerry firmed his shoulders. "That's not the way it works anymore."

"Not the way what works?"

"We are a family now. What bothers you bothers me. If you have a problem, tell me about it, and together, we'll find a way to fix it on account of that's what dads do: they fix things." As the words came out of his mouth, Jerry thought of his own father and how, until recently, the man never tried to fix anything between them. "It's what I do," he corrected.

Max looked up at him with solemn eyes. "I wish you were my real dad, Jerry."

"I may not be your biological father, but we are connected." He considered this for a moment. "Sometimes the gift skips a generation, so technically, we're probably even more connected than if I were."

"I know, but it still would be cool if we had the same last name," she replied.

Jerry was still mulling over those words when they entered the living area. The conversation stopped, and all eyes searched his face for answers.

"Nothing definitive, but Fred said he would try," Jerry said, hoping to ward off an onslaught of questions. Upon seeing the disappointment on both April's and Max's faces, he decided to sweeten the pot. "Fred said if he can't get us on that cruise, he would charter another boat." Okay, so it wouldn't fix the Bigsby problem, but it was better than nothing.

Wayne blew out a long whistle. "That boss of yours either has some mighty deep pockets, or he's pretty liberal with government money."

"Near as I've been able to figure out, the program is specially funded," Jerry said, leaving out that he had no clue where exactly those special funds were coming from.

"It sounds as if we are going on a cruise either way," Lori said, looking on the bright side. Opening a drawer, she brought out a pad of paper and tore off two sheets. She handed one to April and one to Max before offering them each a pen. "Okay, ladies, start making your list."

"What kind of list?" Max asked.

"What you will need to take along on the cruise. The list is to make sure you don't forget anything, since you can't just run to the store to get something you forgot to bring."

"If you forget something, that rich boss of Jerry's can helo it in." Wayne laughed. "Isn't that right, Jer?"

Unsure why his dad seemed to suddenly have an ill opinion of Fred, Jerry remained silent.

"Behave, Wayne. That boss of Jerry's might just leave you off the guest list," Lori said, then offered him a piece of paper.

"It doesn't matter what I write, you'll repack my bags anyway." Wayne's tone held no malice.

"That's because you never pack enough," Lori countered. "You'd be going commando by the third day if I left packing up to you."

Max lifted her pen. "What's 'going commando'?"

"It means your grandmother doesn't think I pack enough underwear," Wayne told her.

Max giggled and lowered her pen once more.

Having no desire to hear any more discussions about his father's underwear, Jerry whistled to get Houdini's attention. "I'm going to take Houdini out and throw the ball to help burn off some of his energy before you leave."

April stood. "Hang on, I'll go with you." She made a show of picking up the paper and waving it toward his mother as she joined him. "I've got my list."

Gunter and Houdini led the way to the front door, running into the side yard that led to the back the second Jerry opened the door. As Gunter nosed the pond, Jerry whistled to get Houdini's attention.

"Are you sure it's safe to leave Max in there?" Jerry asked. "Dad seems to be in rare spirits."

"Max can hold her own," April told him. "She's thirteen. I assure you she was well aware of what 'going commando' meant even before she asked."

"You're saying she was fueling the fire?"

"I'm saying she enjoys being around your family and likes the way they banter."

"You mean argue. I know that can't be easy on you. I guess I should've listened to you and made hotel reservations." Jerry held up the ball for Houdini to see. The dog answered with an eager woof.

"Your parents are great. Don't you dare apologize for them," April responded.

Jerry tossed the ball in the air to get Houdini's attention before slinging it across the yard. A ball lover, Houdini eagerly raced after it and brought it back once more. Jerry tossed it again. "Their squabbling doesn't bother you?"

"You see squabbling. I see two people who care deeply about each other. Trust me, I know arguing." April's cheeks turned crimson. "This is nothing like my relationship with Randy."

"I didn't mean to…"

"I know. I also know you're only looking out for me. Thank you for that."

Deciding this was the right segue, Jerry pressed on. "You've never really mentioned Max's real dad." He tossed the ball once more while waiting to see if April was willing to discuss Max's father.

"That's because there's not much to tell." April grew quiet for a moment, then continued. "I guess if we are going to be married, you should know the rest. Troy was living in his parents' basement when I moved in. His dad was always at the shop, but his mother made it clear she didn't think I was good enough for her son. When I got pregnant, she accused me of doing so on purpose to trap him into marrying me. She must have told him the same thing because he said he was too young to have to worry about raising a kid. He gave me an ultimatum: get rid of it or get out. His mother even offered to pay for the procedure if I agreed to leave Troy alone."

"That was nice of her," Jerry quipped.

"Wasn't it, though? I left him alone, alright, but there was no way I was going to end the pregnancy. I moved back in with my parents. Living there was torture," April sighed, "but even though they never offered to babysit and rarely paid any attention to Max, they never once suggested I should give up my baby. I lived there until I met Randy—another brilliant decision on my part. Anyway, you know the rest."

Jerry was incensed. Even though Max didn't share his DNA, she was a terrific kid, and he couldn't imagine her not being a part of his life. He also felt an even greater love for the woman standing before him and wanted nothing more than to gather her into his arms and thank her for being so brave, but he knew doing so would end their conversation, and he needed more answers. "Troy never tried to see Max?"

"Nope. I reached out to him a couple of times, but he wasn't interested in meeting her. Not having him there was fine, but there were times when some child support would have been nice."

"He never helped out?"

"Not a penny. I could have filed, but my mom said if I pushed the issue, he might insist on visitation or, worse, convince the courts I was unfit and take her from me. It may have been the one bit of sound advice the woman ever gave me."

April wasn't one to talk about her family, so Jerry waited to see if she would say any more.

"She never was much of a grandmother to Max, so I'm surprised she even cared. Max means the world to me, so if you ask me, it is their loss."

"I couldn't agree more," Jerry said, nodding his head. "Any idea where the guy is now?"

"Yep. He has a wife and three kids and is still working in his dad's garage." April laughed, but the humor didn't touch her eyes. "I may have looked him up once just to see. It was after Randy. I guess I just wanted to see what my life could have been if I hadn't left him. It was his life's ambition to take over the shop someday. His dad was older, so he might have passed by now. I'd reckon he'd be too old to work full time in any case."

"And he lives in Detroit?"

"The outskirts. Why all this sudden interest in Max's dad? Are you worried about me having second thoughts about marrying you/ I most definitely am not, but if I were, it wouldn't be because of him."

Tiring of the water, Gunter lowered to the ground, rolled onto his back and wiggled back and forth to scratch an itch. Houdini stopped to sniff Gunter before trotting back to Jerry and dropping the ball at his feet. Jerry obliged him by tossing it once more.

"I was thinking of something Max said," Jerry replied, watching the dog.

"Which was?"

"She said she wished I was her dad."

"You are," April told him. "You've been more of a dad to her than anyone else."

"That's what I told her."

"And?"

"She agreed, then said she wished she had my last name. I get the feeling she thinks she is going to be left out once we get married and you take my last name."

"Who says I will?"

Houdini woofed when Jerry lowered his hand without throwing the ball. "I thought you said you weren't having second thoughts." He tossed the ball when Houdini woofed a second time and picked it up when Houdini brought it back.

"I'm not. I was just kidding. Of course I want to be Mrs. McNeal. Why can't we just change Max's name?"

"I'm not sure that's legal. Even if it were, I would rather make it official." Jerry turned to April as he pocketed the ball. "I want to legally adopt Max."

"Okay."

Though he hadn't anticipated her saying no, the speed at which she agreed took a moment to sink in. "You're okay with it?"

"Sure, why wouldn't I be? Unless," a frown creased her brow, "you have your doubts as to whether our marriage will last."

Though he knew she was serious, he chuckled. "Easy, Ladybug, don't go overthinking the question.

It's a big decision and I only wanted to make sure you gave it some thought."

"I've been doing nothing but think about it since you asked me to marry you, truth be told, and even before that. Not the whole name-change thing, mind you, but the thought of Max having a father she could actually depend on." April bit at her bottom lip before continuing. "I've made a lot of bad decisions in my life, but agreeing to allow you to adopt Max isn't one of them. Plus, if anything happens to me, no one will be able to take her away from you."

"Just you let anyone try," Jerry agreed. "Not that anything will happen to you."

"But if it does."

Jerry placed an index finger on each of his temples and closed his eyes. He opened one eye to see if she was watching, then squeezed it shut once more. "Nope, you're not going anywhere!" he exclaimed, opening them once more.

"You sound pretty sure of yourself, Mr. McNeal," April teased.

Jerry lowered his hands and grinned a wide grin. "Well, I've been told I'm a pretty good psychic."

April giggled.

"You don't believe me?"

April lifted her hand and tapped her index finger toward the body of water that skirted his parents' house. "Did your spidey senses warn you about that?"

Jerry turned, his playfulness abruptly curbed at seeing Gunter and Houdini swimming amongst the reeds. That both dogs were in the water didn't bother him nearly as much as worrying about the alligators that inhabited the ponds around The Villages. He was about to say as much when Max rounded the house in a dead run.

"Houdini!"

Jerry caught her just before she reached the edge of the bank.

"Jerry, there are alligators. I saw them." Her words came in breathless gasps.

Jerry whistled for the dogs. As they turned to answer his call, a large gator popped up a short distance away.

While Jerry knew Gunter could hold his own, he wasn't sure how well Houdini would fare. He bent and started removing his shoes.

"Jerry McNeal, don't you even think about going into that water!" April said firmly. "You'll not make me a widow before we're even married!"

At her words, he knew she was right. Even with Gunter's help, he would be no match for an alligator, especially not in the water. *HELP!* he said, sending a call into the universe.

April gasped, and Jerry realized she, too, could see Clive Tisdale, who'd just appeared on his parents' back lawn.

Sitting high on his horse, he had a lasso in one hand. "I thought you'd never ask. Move back and let ol' Clive show you how it's done."

Not one to argue with a spirit, Jerry took hold of April's and Max's shoulders, the three of them keeping their eyes on Clive, who was now twirling the rope above his head as they backed away from the water's edge.

To Jerry's surprise, the alligator was not the intended target. As the rope slid over Houdini, Clive whistled a shrill whistle before he, his ghostly steed, and both dogs disappeared seconds before the alligator reached the dogs.

"Where'd they go?" April's voice was full of wonder.

Max elbowed him in the ribs and nodded to where Wayne stood with his fingers clamped onto the stucco. Standing next to him, with her mouth agape, his mother was equally pale.

Jerry's cell rang, announcing Fred's call. Keeping his eyes trained on his parents, he dismissed the call while wondering if it would be possible to pass the vision off as an elaborate daydream. Sure, they'd both shared the dream, but if he used some big words and got April and Max to deny seeing anything, it could work. That is, if not for the steaming mound of evidence sitting on the lawn.

Jerry shrugged a helpless shrug. "Got a shovel?"

Chapter Six

Understanding the shock of seeing spirits for the first time, Jerry avoided conversation until everyone was back inside the house. While he knew the dogs were safe with Tisdale, he was relieved to see both Gunter and Houdini waiting for them when they entered the house.

Wayne made a beeline for Houdini, rubbing his hands all over the dog. When he spoke, his voice was filled with wonder. "He's dry! I mean really dry, not just drip dry. Come see," he said, waving Lori over to feel the dog.

Lori knelt, ran her hands through the dog's fur, then gazed at Jerry. "Why, he's dry as a bone! In fact, he smells fantastic." She buried her face in his fur and inhaled. "He smells like he's just been bathed in jasmine. How is that even possible?"

To his relief, both Wayne and Lori ignored Gunter, who was standing next to Houdini wagging his tail, as it meant their seeing Clive had been a fluke of heightened energy.

Jerry's cell rang. He ignored Fred's call a second time. A second later, Max's cell rang. Jerry was still trying to find the answers to his parents' unasked questions; the last thing he wanted was to complicate things. "He can wait," Jerry said, waving her off.

April's phone was the next to ring. She gave Jerry a suffering look. "He's going to send the SWAT team if I don't answer."

April wasn't wrong. Jerry took the phone from her and swiped to answer. "Family emergency. I'll call you back."

"Need me to send someone?"

"Nope." Jerry ended the call without explanation and returned the phone to April as he braced for the barrage of questions to which he would have no real answers.

It was Wayne who finally found his voice. "What was that?"

Jerry decided it was best to keep the answers simple. "Clive Tisdale."

"The Texas Ranger you were telling us about?" Wayne's voice was incredulous.

"That's right," Jerry replied.

Wayne looked at Lori, then leaned back against the sofa. "You mean all those stories you've been telling us are real?"

Jerry laughed for the first time since entering the house. "You doubted me?"

Wayne lifted a brow. "We wanted to believe you, but you have to admit some of them are a little farfetched."

That was putting it lightly. "Dad, I have been able to see spirits since I was a kid. I thought we were past all the doubt."

"Hearing that you see a dog is one thing. As was the little ghost dog pup. But let's face it, we've never actually seen Gunter, and you could have snuck that little pup into the house when we weren't looking just to make sure we believed what you said. But this here man on a horse lassoing a dog in a pond and then disappearing into thin air, that was no illusion. What was he doing here in the first place?"

Okay, when put like that, it did sound a bit surreal. "Clive was saving the dogs from your neighborhood gator."

"Dogs? You mean Gunter was there too?"

"He was." Jerry nodded to where Gunter now lay next to Houdini, basking in the ray of sunlight that streamed in through the sliding glass door. "He's lying next to Houdini."

"Well, if that don't beat all. Though I admit to thinking someone had spiked my morning coffee. I thought I was seeing things, but then your mother said she saw it too. I didn't see Gunter, though. Did you see him, Lori?"

His mother shook her head. "No, I just saw the man and the horse and watched them disappear with the dog." She grew quiet for a moment, then her brows knitted together. "Jerry, where did they disappear to?"

And there was the million-dollar question. "I

have no clue," he said truthfully.

"And they gave him a bath at that," Lori said, continuing her thought. "Do they have grooming salons in heaven?"

Jerry debated telling her Gunter had returned from the other side freshly groomed on more than one occasion but knew doing so would lead to a whole new line of questions. He had enough on his plate than to recant stories of bloody bones whose origins he had no clue and zombie races where Gunter allowed others to both see and photograph him.

"And that horse, if he's dead, how could he leave that on our lawn? It was real. I smelled it!" Lori clutched her hand to her chest. "It's a good thing the neighbors are out of town. Can you imagine having to explain the horse to them?"

"That brings me to my next point," Wayne said, leaning forward once more. "Why were we able to see Clive and his horse? And why them and not Gunter?"

"That's a good question," April said, chiming in. "I saw them too. Just Clive and the horse. I didn't see Gunter."

Okay, this one was a little easier to answer. "I think it was the frequency of the energy. If things are calm, spirits don't always show themselves, but since there was a bit of excitement, then you all were able to see them."

"That time when Clive rescued me from the snake, no one else saw him," Max observed.

Good point, and as such, it shot Jerry's theory down the tube. "Perhaps the only reason everyone saw him today was the man just wanted to show off."

April laughed. "He sure did that!"

"It was a pretty good show," Wayne admitted.

"One I'll not likely forget," Lori agreed.

"I was so scared!" Max cut in. "I was in here talking to Grandma and Gramps, and all of a sudden, I saw the alligator. Not really, just a vision in my mind," she said, clarifying.

"Poor child lit out of here like something was chasing her," Lori told them.

Wayne chuckled. "That she did. It's a good thing that Clive was there, or she'd have probably run right into that pond to save that dog herself."

While his parents were amused by the prospect, Jerry knew they probably weren't far off in their assumption. "It would have been a good way to get yourself killed," Jerry said sternly. "If I have learned anything in dealing with the spirits, it is to ask for help."

"Yes, sir," Max said softly.

April nudged Max with her toe. "Jerry loves you and is just trying to keep you safe."

"I know," Max said.

Jerry's phone rang, announcing Seltzer's call. "I'm going to take this," he said, pushing off the couch.

"Don't forget to call Fred when you're done," April reminded.

Jerry welcomed the reminder. Fred Jefferies was not used to being ignored. "Will do," Jerry said, answering Seltzer's call.

"Sounding a little short there, McNeal. Did I catch you at a bad time?"

That was the thing about Seltzer; the man had a knack for reading his moods. "Do you recall me telling you about that Texas Ranger I met up with a few months back?"

"Cornelius?"

Jerry chuckled. "Close. His name's Clive."

"Clive!" Seltzer mused. "Tisdale, right?"

"That's the one."

"Yeah, what about him?"

"His horse decided to fertilize my parents' yard."

"How do you know it was the ranger's horse?"

"Because Clive was riding it."

"So you're saying your folks saw what he left?"

"I'm saying my folks watched the horse leave it. They saw Clive too, right before he disappeared with my dog."

"The ghost stole Gunter?"

"No, he saved him and Houdini from being eaten by an alligator."

Seltzer snorted into the phone. "McNeal, if I didn't know you better, I'd swear you've been on a binge."

"I wish. If I had been drinking, then I would pass this day off as a really far-out hallucination."

"I hate to be the bearer of bad news, but if you plan on making that pretty lady your wife, your binging days are behind you."

"No worries. I got that all out of my system years ago. I haven't had more than a nightly beer or two in years."

"Good man."

Jerry felt that was a perfect segue. "After I marry April, I plan on formally adopting Max."

"Why do I hear a hint of reservation on your end?"

"It's just this thing with the dogs. I was standing right there talking to April and never once thought about keeping them away from the pond."

"Did you know there were gators in the pond?"

"It's Florida. There are alligators in the bathtubs," Jerry told him. "Seriously, I can't even keep the dogs safe, and here I want to adopt Max and be responsible for her. What was I thinking?"

"Quit beating yourself up, kid. It doesn't matter if you adopted her or helped bring her into the world, things are going to happen. Kids get hurt, or sick, or any number of things. It's what you do about those things that counts. Come to think about it, you may be the perfect father."

"Oh yeah? Why's that?"

"Because it's clear that you have help. Correct me if I'm wrong, but not everyone can summon the ghost of a Texas Ranger to whisk the dogs off to safety or the spirit of their dead grandmother to sing them a lullaby."

Jerry started to tell him that Granny hadn't sung him a lullaby in years when Seltzer continued.

"You're not going to be doing this on your own. You have a whole team, living and dead, ready to step up and protect what is yours. I know because I'm part of that team, and I plan on hanging around. By the way, I want you to know if the big guy calls me early, I'm coming back to haunt you. Imagine the cases we could solve if we were working together."

While Jerry cared for the man, he wasn't sure he was ready for a full-time partner.

Gunter growled.

Present company aside, boy.

Gunter smiled a K-9 smile.

"So, I take it you talked to June?" Jerry asked, reining in the conversation.

"I'm in," Seltzer replied.

"June doesn't have a problem with you going undercover with a beautiful woman?"

"Not when I told her the woman refused to sleep with her victims until after they were married." Laughter floated through the phone. "Of course, she also said if I disrespected her in any way, it would be her doing the killing."

"And she is okay if you have to spend time away from her during the cruise."

"June already considered this a working vacation. Now she won't be the only one working. Plus, she's already writing the scenes," Seltzer informed him.

"I'm not following you."

"The moment I told June what was going on, she got this crazy million-mile stare on her face, and I knew she'd just had another one of her brilliant ideas. I knew better than to ask about it, so I went on and did my thing until she was done. Sure enough, she found me a bit later to show me the rough draft of her plan."

"Her plan?" Jerry wasn't sure he liked the sound of this.

"Yep, she's always wanted to see one of her books come to life, and this way, she'll not only see it, she'll be able to star in her own creation."

Okay, now he knew he didn't like the sound of it. "I'm not so sure I can sign off on having June involved."

"Don't you worry about June. You know I wouldn't do anything to put her in harm's way. She will just be there for the theatrics. When the time's right, she'll make a big scene and break up with her money bags; that's me. There will be words said that will leave no doubt that I'm loaded and fresh for the picking."

"I don't know…"

"McNeal, it's a solid plan, and unless you'll be on the cruise, it's the only one you've got."

The man had a point. "Okay, let me run it up the chain and see what the boss thinks."

"If he's smart, he'll think it's brilliant," Seltzer replied.

"I'll be in touch." Jerry disconnected the call, then braced himself for another round of questions as he dialed Fred.

"McNeal? Everything okay?" Fred's normally

calm voice was full of concern.

Deciding there was no use beating around the bush, Jerry decided to tell the man of the morning's excitement. To his credit, Fred refrained from commenting until Jerry finished relating the sequence of events. Even then, he was slow to respond. Then again, it was no secret that while Fred Jefferies believed in spirits, he himself had never actually seen one.

"I take it there are no cameras on the outside of your parents' home?"

"Nope."

"Would they be opposed to having some installed?"

Jerry started to remind him that the chances of a repeat performance were slim to none, as was the possibility of actually capturing a spirit on camera. Then again, his parents weren't getting any younger, and he wouldn't mind having extra eyes on them. "I would have to ask, but only on the outside perimeter. You don't want cameras inside the courtyard."

"You mean you don't," Fred clarified.

"No, I mean you. There are stone walls around the pool, and my mother fully trusts those walls to keep gawkers at bay. My mother is not a spring chicken," Jerry said when Fred didn't answer.

"Now, I'm reading you," Fred replied. "Thanks for the heads-up. I assure you the agency will respect your parents' privacy."

"Says the man asking to put up cameras around their house."

"How did April take the news?" Fred asked, ignoring the comment.

"News?"

"About coming to work for the agency? You did tell her?"

"To be honest, in all the excitement, I completely forgot to say anything. Is that what you were calling about earlier?" Jerry asked, suddenly reminded of the fact Fred had called three times.

"No, I was calling to let you know I am still working on getting you and the family on that ship, but I have a yacht on standby if that doesn't pan out. Or, we have the jet and can at least get you to Mexico to meet the ship."

Jerry sighed, knowing his chance of convincing April to have a cruise ship wedding was slipping away.

"You talk to Seltzer about keeping an eye on those two while on the ship?"

"I did. Seltzer thinks he may have devised a plan to get her looking in his direction," Jerry said without disclosing June's involvement.

"I like it."

"You haven't even heard the plan."

"Don't need to. The guy didn't move up the chain without having some smarts to back him up. Besides, he's a much better catch than you."

Okay, Jerry liked Seltzer and all, but the thought of him being a better catch was a bit too much to take. "I'm not sure how I feel about that."

"Don't go letting your ego get the best of you,"

Fred said. "This woman is not looking for a soul mate. She's looking for someone who won't raise suspicion if he is suddenly killed off."

Okay, put like that, the choice made perfect sense.

"We'll get your man some fake credentials and even a phony medical record. We'll keep their first names the same to keep things simple. It probably wouldn't be bad to have him see the ship's doctor once on board to further the ruse."

"I'll have April set him up a fake social media account," Jerry replied.

"We have people for that," Fred told him.

"And now you have April. Don't forget that it was her computer sleuthing skills that were instrumental in flushing out the Hash Mark Killer. April is one of the smartest people I've ever met when it comes to a computer. Besides, it'll make her happy knowing she's doing something to earn the money you're going to pay her."

"Weave it however you want, and I'll sign off on it."

"Before you hang up, I have another favor to ask."

Fred chuckled. "How much is this one going to cost me?"

"Nothing. I'll foot the bill if you can get it done."

"Go on."

"I want to legally adopt Max. However, that means contacting Max's biological father and encouraging him to relinquish his parental rights. I was planning on doing it, but it might go over better coming from an outside source. It should be easy, as the man has never shown any interest in meeting her. According to April, he lives just outside of Detroit."

"I know where he lives," Fred replied.

That comment didn't come as a surprise, as Fred Jefferies left nothing to chance.

"Don't worry, I'll have my guys make him an offer he can't refuse. What's so funny?" Fred asked when Jerry laughed.

"For a moment, I thought I was speaking with Mario Fabel. The guy seems to like me. Perhaps I should have put him on the case," Jerry said, referring to the mobster who had taken a special interest in him after he and Gunter had helped track down his sister's killer.

"You ask a favor of Mario Fabel, be prepared to give one in return," Fred warned.

"Don't worry, that's one rock I don't plan on turning over," Jerry said, disconnecting the call.

Chapter Seven

April

April looked at her watch, calculating the time needed to drive back to The Villages. Even with stopping to eat, she should still have plenty of time to take a shower and start creating fake profiles for both Brian and June. Though Jerry had only requested one for Brian, anyone worth their salt would not check out his profile without also checking out the competition. He wasn't worried about creating a friends list for either of them, as she could lock that down so that no one could see they didn't have any. As soon as Jerry told her of the plan, she'd messaged June with a request for photos, which she planned to use to populate the profile. The trick would be to manipulate the account so that it didn't look like a completely new account—easy to do if someone had the know-how, which she did.

As she shopped, she formed a plan in her mind. It helped that Lori lived in Florida year-round and already had most of the things she needed for the trip. After getting the things on her list, she then whisked Max off to gather things for her, giving April the rare opportunity to shop on her own. It wasn't that she minded shopping with Max. She'd been doing so for thirteen years. Still, it was nice to pick out an outfit without an opinionated eyeroll causing her to second-guess her choice.

As if to prove the point, April snagged several outfits from the rack and took them along with three bathing suits to the dressing room, where she alone would decide whether or not to buy them.

She stripped out of her clothes and tried on the first outfit, white shorts, and a yellow top, twisting back and forth to measure the fit. Deciding it was a keeper, she moved on to the next outfit and found it to be a perfect fit as well. It was the same for the next and all three bathing suits. She couldn't recall when she'd had so much fun trying on clothes.

Not that anything could bring her down today.

Not only was she one day closer to becoming Mrs. Jerry McNeal—if she could settle on a wedding date. But she was also officially one of the team. Not just the Jerry McNeal team, but THE TEAM.

As she removed the final bathing suit and retrieved the sundress she'd worn into the room, she giggled aloud as she recalled the conversation with Jerry and her stunned reaction to hearing Fred had offered her a place within the agency. Granted, it would've been cool to hear it from Jefferies himself, but that wasn't the point. She was working with the …okay, she hadn't a clue which agency it really was, but she'd get a badge.

Will I get a gun?

She glanced in the mirror at the dress she was now wearing, wondering where she'd put it, and further wondered if she'd have to rethink her wardrobe. *Will I even need a gun? Jerry carries one. Perhaps they will issue me one as well. Of course, Jerry would have to teach me how to use it.* April stared at her image in the triple mirrors within the dressing room. Picking up her cell phone, she flashed it like a badge. "April Buchanan, Department of Defense." Not bad, but it was missing something. She flashed the imaginary badge once more. "April McNeal, Department of Defense."

Much better.

A giddiness raced through her the likes of which she'd never felt. While she wanted nothing more than to shout her good fortune to the world, she took several breaths to calm herself as she studied her image once more. *Look how far you've come. Less than two years ago, you were scrimping for every penny and wondering how you were going to afford to fill the fuel oil tank to keep you and your daughter from freezing to death.* A chill raced along her arms as she remembered. *Now look at you with a super sexy fiancé, building your dream home, future in-laws that actually like you and a promise of a six-figure income!*

How is this my life?!

April's gaze slid from the packages piled high in the single chair that occupied the room to the outfits she now intended to buy. Feeling an overabundance of excited energy, she squeezed her eyes closed and did a silent celebratory dance. Opening her eyes, she pinched herself to ensure it wasn't all just a wonderful dream. According to the red mark on her forearm, it wasn't. She closed her eyes, hugging her arms to her chest, silently squealing and feeling like Julia Roberts in the bathtub during one of the scenes in the movie *Pretty Woman.*

It's real!

"My wife is in danger, and you're in here playing dress-up." Both the menace in Bigsby's voice and the fact she could actually see him sent a chill up April's spine.

April took a step back as Bigsby moved closer, standing between her and the door. "You forgot to add hearing spirits to your list. Or did you forget you are supposed to be helping us?"

It took her a moment to fully grasp his words and the fact he'd been listening to her unspoken words. She hurried to block him. "I didn't forget."

"Yeah, well, it looks like it to me. You're trembling. Go ahead and scream. Tell whoever comes to your rescue you were frightened by a ghost."

"I'm not afraid," she lied. In fact, she was terrified, but if she was going to be working for the agency, she needed to put on a brave front. *Think, April. What would Jerry do? For starters, he wouldn't let the spirit get the upper hand.* She worked to keep her voice even. "Mr. Bigsby. You need to leave."

"I'm not leaving until you help my wife," Bigsby hissed.

Before she had a chance to react, Gunter appeared.

Wearing his K-9 police vest, he stood between her and the spirit—his deep growl filling the small space.

Bigsby disappeared as April's phone rang, announcing Jerry's call.

"I'm okay," April said, answering the call. "Gunter's here."

"You don't sound okay. What happened?"

"Hang on; Max is calling." April switched the call. "I'm okay. I'm on the phone with Jerry and Gunter's here."

"I got scared," Max replied. "Where are you?"

"I'm okay. I need to talk to Jerry, then I'll come to you. Okay?"

"Okay, Mom. We're in the food court."

"Stay there. I'll come find you as soon as I'm done." April switched the call to Jerry. "Sorry. Max was worried. Anyway, Mr. Bigsby was here, then Gunter came and scared him away."

"You saw him?"

April wasn't sure which him Jerry was referring to. "I saw them both. Mr. Bigsby wasn't happy, then Gunter showed up. He was wearing his vest. Jerry, didn't you say he only does that when he senses a threat?"

"He wears the vest when he's working. Is he still

with you?"

"I think so. I can't see him, but I can feel him."

"Good."

"Why good?"

"If you can't see him, it means the threat is gone. Did anyone else see him?"

"No, I'm in the dressing room."

"Max and Houdini aren't with you?"

"It's a small dressing room."

"If Houdini isn't there, it explains why Gunter showed up."

"I'm glad he did."

"Are you sure you're okay?"

"A little shaken up," she admitted. "He heard my thoughts. I blocked him the moment I realized it, but I didn't know he was here. How am I supposed to block him when I don't know he's here?"

"If he was there, you probably missed the sign. You're new to this, April. These things will come with time and experience."

"I wish there was an instruction manual I could read."

"Just listen to your gut. A sudden unease, smell, a chill."

"That's it! I felt a chill but didn't realize what it was."

"That was probably when he showed up," Jerry told her. "How's the shopping trip?"

April laughed. "You mean besides Mr. Bigsby?"

"Yes, besides that. Are you finding everything you need?"

April looked at her mound of bags. "I may have gone a little overboard."

"Better to do it now than after we get on the ship."

April giggled at the joke.

"Wish I was there to carry your bags."

"If you were here, you'd have your own bags to carry," she said, speaking to the fact Jerry shopped like a girl. "I wish you would have come."

"So do I, but I didn't want to deprive Mom of her girls' day out. Hey, Gunter's with you, so I doubt you'll have to worry about Mr. Bigsby," Jerry said.

"Okay, I'm going to pay for my stuff and go find Max."

"Love you, Ladybug."

"I love you too, Jerry." April held on to the phone a few more seconds before finally disconnecting the call. She debated leaving without making her purchase, then decided against it. Mr. Bigsby was not going to ruin her good mood.

***

While April could no longer see Gunter, she could feel his presence as she made her way to the food court. By the time she reached her daughter, her nerves were under control.

The same couldn't be said for Max, who ran to greet her the moment she came into view. Houdini stayed at her side as Max searched her, presumably for injuries. "Mom, what happened?"

"Mr. Bigsby paid me a visit. Don't worry, he just wanted to talk."

"I don't believe you," Max replied. "If all he wanted was to talk, Gunter wouldn't be here."

Busted.

April pressed some of the bags into her daughter's hands. "You're right. He's not happy I haven't helped his wife. Does your grandmother know?"

"No, you and Jerry said we shouldn't worry them."

"Okay, good. Do you see Mr. Bigsby?" April held her breath.

"No."

April breathed a sigh of relief. While she hadn't felt the spirit, it was good to have confirmation. "See, Gunter scared him off. Come on, keep walking. We don't want to worry your grandmother."

"Looks like you've had a productive day," Lori said when she reached the table. "Did you have fun?"

"It was quite exhilarating," April said, winking at Max.

Lori looked at her watch. "Good, we should just about make it."

"To where?" April asked.

"You'll see," Lori said, evading the question.

April worked to hide her disappointment. While she was calm, she wanted nothing more than to get back to Jerry. "You didn't find everything you were looking for?"

Lori hoisted her bags. "Just humor me."

***

It was a thirty-minute drive to the next stop, with Lori chatting away about nothing in particular and Max deep in thought as she sketched in her sketchbook. April might have enjoyed the ride more if not for thinking of Bigsby and wishing she'd brought her computer so she could begin work on the social media pages. As it was, instead of heading back toward The Villages, they seemed to be on a secret mission.

April discovered the reason for the secrecy the moment Lori pulled into the parking lot. If she'd known the location, she would have declined. While the building itself was nondescript, the sign on the door, along with the white gowns lining the front windows, showed this to be a wedding boutique.

"Here we are," Lori said, putting her car into park. "I'm sorry to have bushwacked you like this, but if I would have told you, I'm pretty sure you would have said no."

Bushwack was right; up until this moment, Lori had not made a single mention of the engagement. "You're not wrong," April said dryly.

Lori unbuckled her seatbelt and turned to face her. "Please don't be mad."

"I'm not mad," April said truthfully. "I just wasn't expecting this. To be honest, I haven't decided what kind of wedding I want, much less what I'll wear."

Lori looked over the seat at Max as if debating her next move. Seeming to come to a decision, she turned in April's direction once more. "Jerry is hoping to convince you to marry him."

"He doesn't have to convince me to marry him. I've already agreed."

"No, dear," Lori clarified. "Convince you to marry him on the ship, by the ship's captain."

April swallowed. "He told you that?"

"No," Lori said. "Max overheard Jerry on the phone talking to Brian."

"I wasn't spying on him. I was in the hall and heard him. He doesn't know I know."

April frowned. "Why hasn't he said anything?"

"Probably because he didn't want to get your hopes up if his boss can't get us on the cruise. Jerry told us you didn't want a big wedding, but I'm not going to lie, I would love to be there when my boy gets married."

Great, Lori was playing the mom card. It wasn't that April was opposed to getting married on the ship, but wearing a wedding gown seemed a little extravagant since it wasn't her first marriage. Then again, she and Randy had said their vows at the courthouse; maybe she did deserve a little something different this time. A ship wedding might not be a bad compromise. "I guess it wouldn't hurt just to take a look around."

"Atta girl," Lori said, opening the door.

"I have the final say," April whispered as Max and Houdini filed out of the backseat. "No ganging up on me, or I'll make you wear pink."

"It's okay, Mom, you have good taste in clothes.

I know you'll find the perfect dress. And I don't mind wearing pink. In fact, Grandma bought me a dress."

April placed her palm on Max's forehead. "Are you feeling okay?"

Max giggled.

"No fever," April continued. "I think Maxine showed up today. Max wouldn't be caught dead wearing pink."

"It will be your special day," Max told her. "I'll wear whatever you want. I just want you to be happy."

"Us," April said, holding the door. "I want us to be happy."

Whether from the racks of dresses, the tiered stage surrounded by mirrors, or the simple fact that being here meant she was one step closer to marrying Jerry, the moment April stepped inside the bridal showroom, something changed.

A small-framed woman with white hair entered the room and clapped her hands to get their attention. "You have this room booked for ninety minutes. My name is Charlene, but you can call me Char. Time's a-wasting, so let's get started."

"Ninety minutes?"

Lori shrugged. "It was all the time they have available tonight."

"Yes, we usually like more time for the fittings, but since you'll be buying off the rack, that should be plenty of time." Char pulled out a cloth tape measure, started in April's direction then came to an abrupt stop. Frowning, she altered her approach only to stop for a second time, almost as if hitting an invisible wall.

April was about to ask if she was okay when Max clapped the side of her leg. To anyone else, it would look like an innocent gesture, but April knew it for what it was—she was telling Gunter to stand down. April gave the girl a grateful smile as the woman moved closer and wrapped the tape around her bosom.

After several more measurements and some quick calculations, Char nodded. "Now tell me about the perfect dress."

April frowned. "I haven't given it much thought."

Char made a tsking sound with her tongue and pulled out a binder full of photos and began slowly flipping through the pages.

April studied each page, picturing herself in the dress then shaking her head. Too formal. Too much lace. Too long of a train. Too low cut. While the dresses were beautiful, April found herself feeling like Goldilocks and further wondered if agreeing to do this was a mistake.

"No, don't go getting discouraged. This is my method for ruling out what you don't want in order to save time." Char set the book aside and pulled out another, repeating the process. "It's in here," she said as she lifted the fourth book.

"How can you be so sure?" Max asked.

"Simple, it's the last one," Char said, peeling

back the cover.

Six pages into the fourth book, April saw it. Feminine, playful, elegant enough for the red carpet and billowy enough for an ocean cruise, it was perfect in every way. Wide lace straps held up the formfitting lace bodice, which showed enough cleavage to be alluring without looking trashy, and continued into a large keyhole cutout in the back. The lace stopped at the waist and flowed into a lightweight, billowy chiffon, which would show off the hips and bottom without clinging. If not for the need to ensure the fit, April wouldn't have felt the need to try it on. Then again, perhaps she was just nervous about being alone in the dressing room, a null point when Char followed her inside and helped her into the dress.

Char's gaze traveled the length of her as she walked around her several times tugging and pressing the fabric. "It fits like it was made special for you."

"It's beautiful," April agreed.

"No, it's just a dress; it is you who makes it beautiful. Now go, show your mother. I will return shortly," Char said before April could correct her.

April pulled aside the curtain and stepped onto the stage, waiting for Max and Lori to notice.

Houdini yipped.

Max looked up and offered a wide smile as she raised both thumbs to show her approval.

Lori's jaw dropped then morphed into a bewildered stare.

April smoothed the dress with her hands as she studied the woman. "You don't like it?"

"It's beautiful."

"But?"

Lori nodded to Max. "Show her."

Max shrugged off her backpack and pulled out her sketchbook.

If April had had any doubt, it was now gone, as Max had sketched a perfect rendition of her wearing the exact dress. The only difference in the photo was April's hair was pulled up and the background, which clearly showed the upper deck of a ship.

"How?" Lori's question floated through the air.

"I have no idea," April answered honestly.

"So, is this the one?" Char asked, returning to the room.

"Yes," April said, confirming the choice.

"The dress is on me and Wayne," Lori told her.

"I can't let you do that," April argued.

"You can and you will." Lori smiled. "Besides, this way, you won't have to lie to Jerry when he asks if you bought yourself anything special."

Chapter Eight

Jerry

Jerry balled his fingers into fists as he paced the courtyard around his parents' pool. While he didn't consider himself to be a hothead, at the moment, he fervently wished Bigsby was alive, as he wanted more than anything to give him a good beating. The spirit had overstepped the spiritual boundaries by not only frightening April but doing so after asking for her help.

That was low rent, living or dead.

That Gunter hadn't returned made him both grateful and slightly concerned. The question was, did Gunter stay merely to calm her, or did he still feel the spirit lingering nearby?

The sliding door opened, and Wayne stepped outside carrying two bottles of Bud. He offered one to Jerry.

Jerry relaxed his fingers as he accepted the beverage. "Thanks, Pop."

"Boy, you're going to wear a hole in the concrete

with all that pacing. You act like you've never let them out of your sight before. Do you want some company? I could go back inside if you'd rather keep pacing."

"Wouldn't be very nice of me running you out of your own backyard now, would it?" Jerry stepped aside, followed Wayne to the outdoor living room, and sat in the chair across from him.

"Care to tell me what's on your mind?" Wayne pulled a paper towel from his pocket. He placed it on the couch beside him, then thumbed it open to unveil a cookie.

"Gunter's not here. April had a visit from Bigsby."

"That's the ghost you and she are trying to help?" Wayne asked, pocketing the cookie once more.

"Spirit, and yes, that's the one." Jerry rubbed his thumb around the lip of the bottle. "Showed up while she was alone in the dressing room."

"The dog went to scare him away?"

"More to let him know April is under his protection."

"What would have happened if Gunter hadn't shown up?"

Jerry lifted the bottle and took a long swallow before answering. "I don't know."

"You think the spirit is dangerous?"

"I didn't, but April said Gunter was wearing his vest, so that means the spirit's energy is escalating."

"April doesn't normally see them, so that means the dog's energy must have been palpable," Wayne mused.

"You've been paying attention."

"Something I should have done thirty years ago."

While Jerry wanted to agree, doing so wouldn't change anything. "Water under the bridge."

"Why a dog?" Wayne asked after a long silence.

"Why a dog what?"

"You have all kinds of spirits helping you, so why settle for a dog?"

Jerry drained his bottle and sat it on the side table. "First, I didn't settle, and second, why not a dog?"

"Don't get riled. I didn't mean nothing by it. I'm just trying to have one of those conversations we should have had years ago. I'm just asking why have a dog when you could have the ghost of a Texas Ranger following you around. I mean, you can talk to him, and from what you've said, he'd likely answer you back."

"I didn't choose Gunter; he chose me," Jerry replied. "Clive is here when I need him."

"I just never saw you as a dog person." Wayne's voice held an edge.

"Maybe that's because you wouldn't let us have a dog," Jerry said, matching his tone.

"Wasn't going to chance getting attached to another one after we had to get rid of Tippy."

"Tippy?"

"Great dog. Had him before you were even born. 'Bout broke your mother's heart to send him away."

Joseph appeared on the couch beside Wayne. His

brother shook his head. "He's lying. The dog was Dad's."

Jerry debated telling his father Joseph was sitting beside him, then realized no good would come in him knowing and decided against it.

"You don't think he can handle knowing I'm a ghost?" Joseph tickled his father's ear with his finger, laughing when the man attempted to swat his hand away.

"I don't remember having a dog," Jerry said, drawing his father's attention.

"He didn't like you."

Jerry searched his father's face, wondering if he'd heard correctly. "What?"

"I said we had to get rid of the dog because he didn't like you. At first, we thought he was jealous of you since you were a newborn and getting all our attention, but then, once you started walking, he'd follow you around and growl. Or wake us all up barking at you. It was your mother's idea to get rid of him; she was afraid he'd bite you."

"Dad loved that dog," Joseph told him.

"I'm sorry."

"Water under the bridge," Wayne said, throwing his words back at him. "Betty Lou was upset when we told her, claiming the dog was trying to protect you, not hurt you. Said you must have some evil spirits lingering around. She was always spewing stuff like that."

"But not you, Dad. You didn't believe in crap like that." Joseph pulled his arm back and rested his hand on Wayne's leg.

As if feeling the touch, Wayne placed his hand on top of Joseph's.

Joseph pulled his hand away and placed it on top of Wayne's once more, then chortled when Wayne lifted his and placed it on top once more. "You should tell him, Jer."

"What kind of dog?" Jerry asked, ignoring his brother's antics.

A yellow lab appeared on the seat next to his father.

"Yellow lab," Wayne confirmed. "Good dog. I hated to see him go. Probably one of the worst decisions I ever made."

"Ask him why," Joseph urged.

"Why's that?"

"Because we traded the dog for imaginary friends."

A chill raced along the back of Jerry's neck. "You thought the spirits were my imaginary friends?"

Joseph pulled a bell from his pocket. "Ding, ding, give the man a prize."

"I thought you were just missing the dog. We let it go for a while; then, I would get after you anytime you said anything. It worked for a while."

Joseph laughed a wicked laugh. "That's when Aunt Edna showed up."

"Then you had to get your brother involved."

Jerry's chill spread. "What's Joseph have to do with this?"

"Because I saw her too," Joseph said. "Boy, we

sure gave old Pop a near stroke with that one."

"He was parroting you. It was bad enough when you claimed to talk to people who weren't there, but when your imagination started affecting Joseph, I knew something had to be done."

"No, Joseph was scared of seeing her body. I remember he shut down and didn't talk for a week."

"It wasn't Aunt Edna who scared me. It was Pop," Joseph clarified. "Don't be too hard on the old man, Jer. He has lived with his guilt for much too long."

"I lit into him. I don't recall exactly what I said, but it worked, as he never mentioned it again." There was deep remorse in Wayne's voice.

All those years of taking the blame for things his brother had done, and all along, Joseph was responsible for his own actions. Jerry swallowed. "Joseph had the gift?"

"Nah, I couldn't tell when something was going to happen. I just saw spirits for a while."

Wayne's shoulders slumped. "I don't know what he had, but I cured him of it. At least that's the way I looked at it. I treated you wrong, son, and have lived with those regrets for years. If I could go back and change things, I would," he said as if he somehow sensed Joseph's presence and was hoping to make amends to them both.

"He's got a guilty conscience," Joseph said. "You need to let him off the hook, bro."

A sadness touched Jerry's heart as he wondered how much different their lives would have been if

Joseph had been allowed to nurture his gift. While he should have been angry at his father, he felt the man's pain, and all he felt was a deep sorrow for what could have been. Jerry pushed aside his own grief. "We've talked about things before. Why are you just sharing this with me now?"

"I've been thinking of your Ranger friend. He came along and helped you when you needed it." Wayne's eyes misted. "I was thinking if I hadn't cured Joseph of his imaginary friends that perhaps he would have had help that day."

"Hey, Pop, I understand that guilt. I lived with it for years. Joseph's death is not on you. You said it before: it was Joseph's time. He would have most likely died that day, no matter the circumstances."

"Most likely."

"I don't have all the answers, Pop." Jerry sighed. "The truth is we'll never know."

"I don't deserve your forgiveness, and before you go saying it's water under the bridge, just know at some point that creek is going to overflow."

"Make it up to me…"

"Us," Joseph said before he could finish.

"Us," Jerry corrected. "Make it up to me and Joseph by always being there for Max."

"Max is a great kid. Do you think you and April will have any of your own?"

"If we do, I wouldn't love the baby any more than I love Max."

"You're a good man, Jerry. I'm not sure if I've ever said it, but I'm proud of you, son. Not because you can see spirits, but because despite my best efforts, you've turned out to be a good man. I wouldn't fault you for not wanting Max to be around me, but I am grateful that you are allowing me to make up for the errors of my past."

"Max has had a lot of disappointment in her life. I wouldn't have brought her here if I didn't feel you'd changed."

"I know that 'thank you' isn't much of a sentiment, but it's all I have."

"It's enough, Pop," Jerry said, looking past him at Joseph, who was nodding his agreement. "If Joseph were here, he'd agree."

Jerry remained in the courtyard long after his father went inside, digesting all he'd learned. He was glad he hadn't learned of Joseph's gift earlier, as a younger version of himself would not have handled the knowledge as well. What now felt like closure could have easily driven a deeper wedge between him and his father. As it was, it was just one more piece of the puzzle that had plagued him throughout his life. His father hadn't hated him; he'd sacrificed him to save his other son. While being allowed to live with his grandmother placed a distance between him and his parents, it could have been much worse.

His phone rang, announcing Fred's call. Jerry answered.

"Pack your bags, McNeal. You're going on a cruise."

"And the family?"

"Them too. Three rooms close together, just like you requested. If you need any more, just let me know."

Jerry welcomed the good news. "Dare I ask how you accomplished this?"

"I wish I could take credit, but this might be more up your alley."

"How's that?"

"Ten minutes ago, I was prepared to pick up the phone to tell you it couldn't be done. As I was reaching for the phone, my contact at the cruise line called to tell me an entire wedding party had canceled."

"Cold feet?"

"Food poisoning from eating raw fish. Never had a taste for sushi myself, and this firms up my decision not to partake. Anyway, under normal circumstances, it would be too late to get you and the family on board, but as you know, I have all the cool phone numbers. Sit tight. I'll have a messenger bring you a packet with all the particulars," Fred said, disconnecting the call.

Jerry sat and placed his elbows on the table, intertwining his fingers. Resting his forehead on his thumbs, he allowed the emotions of the day to run their course.

***

Not wanting any surprises, Jerry decided it was best to speak to Bigsby before stepping foot on the ship. He further surmised it would be best to do so when April, Max and the dogs were present. While he'd originally thought to leave Max out of it, he knew with the added protection of Gunter and Houdini, it would be a safe learning environment for both her and April.

Jerry glanced at Max, the epitome of calm, as she sat cross-legged on the couch with her sketchbook at the ready. She saw him looking and gave him a thumbs-up. God, how he loved that kid and admired her ability to roll with the punches.

He sent Max a wink and then turned his attention to April, who, while putting on a brave face, was trembling. He took her in his arms, hoping to absorb some of her fear. "It's okay, April. Both Houdini and Gunter are here."

"I can't see Gunter," she told him. "Is that a good thing?"

Don't lie to her, McNeal. Jerry released his hold and nodded to where Gunter stood. "Yes and no. He's here, and he's wearing his vest, but that could just be because he knows we're about to go to work. Keep in mind if Bigsby's energy changes, you will probably see Gunter. Don't let that scare you, as I'll be surprised if it doesn't happen. Spirits are afraid of him, and this is Gunter's way of letting them know they have a reason to be afraid. This is all to say, the dogs have our back and getting everything out in the open should settle his spirit so we don't have to worry about Bigsby cornering you again."

"I understand."

Jerry gave April a moment to steady herself. "Are you ready?"

April nodded.

"Take your time and remember to block him from reading you. Call him when you're ready."

April spread her fingers and pushed her hands across her body as if releasing her nervous energy. Pulling herself taller, she called into the night, "Mr. Bigsby, a word, if you please."

Jerry felt a tingle on the back of his neck as Bigsby appeared. April nodded, indicating she could see him.

Balding and wearing a dark suit, the spirit eyed the dogs, who were leaning forward with tails and ears erect, obviously ready to intervene if he got out of line. "Call off your hounds."

"We have a matter to discuss with you," Jerry replied. "The dogs won't bother you unless you give them a reason."

"I hope you called me here to tell me of your plan to protect my wife."

As they'd discussed, April took the lead. "We will be on the cruise and will be watching your wife."

"Why not just go to her and tell her all I've said?"

"Because we believe there is more to the story."

"What do you mean more?" Waves rippled across his parents' swimming pool even though the air was still.

April glanced at Gunter, indicating the dog was now visible to her. "We believe your wife killed you and the man she was married to before. We further believe she plans on killing her new husband after they get married as well."

"That is preposterous!" Bigsby said then took a step back when both dogs growled. "Don't you think I would know if I were murdered?"

"Maybe. Maybe not," Jerry said. "It wouldn't be the first time I've come across a spirit with amnesia. It could be that you don't know, or it's quite possible you are blocking that knowledge. Either way, we have a plan to find out."

"What kind of plan?"

"We will have someone on board who will try to get close to your wife and get her to play her hand."

"And what if I'm right and this con man decides to play his hand first?"

"Jerry and I will be there to make sure he doesn't hurt her," April assured him. "And if the man is who you say he is, we'll get him too."

"What about the dogs?"

"They will be there too," Jerry said, "to make sure everyone is playing fair. This includes you, which means no whispering in your wife's ear."

"Mr. Bigsby, I promise we are not making this up, and if she is responsible for your death, Jerry said it could be why you are stuck here." April softened her tone. "Isn't it best you know the truth?"

"What will happen to her if you're right?" Bigsby asked.

"She'll be arrested," Jerry told him. "And then you'll be free to move on."

Bigsby's energy grew calm. "I won't interfere."

"That went well," April said when Bigsby

disappeared. "Do you think he'll really move on if his wife is found guilty?"

"I don't know, but if that is what's keeping him here, the knowing should release the hold." Jerry looked over at Max, who was intently sketching in her book. "Whatcha working on, kiddo?"

Max held up a finger then turned the pad around a few moments later.

While he'd expected to see a drawing of him and April speaking with Bigsby, the image showed Jerry sitting, leaning forward in his chair, speaking with his father. Although it was still a rough sketch, Jerry could clearly see Joseph sitting next to the man, his arm casually draped around his shoulder. On the man's other side sat a large Labrador retriever.

Tippy.

A chill raced along Jerry's spine as he studied the drawing. While he had listened to them tell of their shopping trip and discussed how they were going to deal with Bigsby, he had not yet had time to tell either of them about the discussion with his father.

Chapter Nine

Jerry

Jerry pulled to a stop at the terminal, and Max squealed over his shoulder for at least the hundredth time since first spying the ships in the distance. "I can't believe we're really going on a cruise!" she shouted as Houdini joined in the chorus.

"Max, honey, I know you're excited, but try not to yell and please quiet Houdini before he gives your grandparents a heart attack."

"Sorry. Easy, Houdini, no speak," Max said, shushing the dog. "I'm just so excited."

"Oh, let the girl have her fun," Wayne said. "I'd scream like a schoolgirl myself if I didn't think Jerry would think me a fool."

"Go ahead, Pop," Jerry urged.

"Please don't encourage them," April said. "You know Houdini feeds off her energy. The last thing we want is to draw unnecessary attention to him."

"I thought you said he was cleared for traveling on the ship," Lori replied.

"He's cleared for traveling everywhere," Jerry said. "April's worried someone will have something to say about him being on the ship."

"If they do, tell them to mind their own beeswax," Wayne scoffed.

Jerry got out and began unloading the bags. While it had been his idea to leave them near the pier while he parked and met with Seltzer, he was now having second thoughts about leaving April to deal with everything.

"I see that worried look. We will be fine," April said, joining him at the back of the SUV. "You go meet with Brian, and I'll look after your parents. As soon as we turn over our baggage to the porter, we'll get in line. From the looks of that line, it could take hours to actually get on board. I promise to text you if it looks like it's moving quicker."

Jerry pulled her in for a hug. "Where have you been all of my life?"

April smiled. "Waiting for you to come rescue me."

"I'm afraid you have that backward; it was you who rescued me." Jerry gave her a quick kiss before releasing her. "Any word from Bigsby?"

April shook her head. "No. Why? Do you see him?"

"No, he's probably staying close to his wife." Jerry nodded to the bow of the ship. "Granny and Bunny are already onboard."

"According to Max, they are just as excited about this cruise as we are." April frowned. "Max thinks

Granny and Bunny were behind the food poisoning. I mean, I wanted to go and all, but that poor woman had to miss her wedding. Do you really think they had something to do with us getting onboard?"

"I'd place money on it. Up until that moment, even Fred couldn't get us all on. Then again, it was a joint effort with both in-laws preparing the food, and no one died. Listen, things could definitely be worse. Please don't let it spoil your trip. I've got to go. I'll join you as soon as I can." He gave her a quick peck and looked at Gunter. "Ready to roll?"

In answer to his question, Gunter disappeared and reappeared in the passenger seat.

Though his father had voiced his concern about leaving the heavily loaded SUV unattended in an unknown area, Jerry wasn't worried, The Durango was equipped with stealth technology from both the agency and his spirit companions who'd watched over the SUV on more than one occasion. As an added precaution, Jerry parked in sight of a camera, knowing the agency would hack into it to further monitor the SUV.

"Okay, I wouldn't be opposed to someone watching over the Durango while we are away," he said to the unknown before turning to Gunter. "Ready to find Seltzer?"

Gunter answered with an enthusiastic bark and disappeared.

Jerry smiled when the dog appeared at the driver's door. Though he could have easily called to find the location or easily used his own ability to find him, he knew Gunter would streamline the search. While their plan was mostly ironed out, Jerry planned to go over it one last time when he handed over the packet the courier had dropped off in the middle of the night. Since he hadn't seen his friend since he and April had gotten together, he also wanted to sneak in a greeting before Seltzer went undercover.

Gunter spun in a circle as Jerry slid out of the driver's seat and then took off toward the back of the parking structure. Jerry followed as the ghostly K-9 weaved a path in and around parked cars before stopping in front of a black pickup truck. Backed into the space, Jerry was able to see June sitting in the front of the cab with her laptop open in her lap. What he didn't expect to see was Bunny and Granny sitting next to her in the cab. While Granny looked up and offered him a finger wave, Bunny was too busy whispering in June's ear to notice him. Whatever the spirit was saying must have been good, as June's fingers were a blur. Deciding to leave them to it, Jerry crept to the back of the truck, where Seltzer stood gazing at the screen of his cell phone. Jerry cleared his throat.

Instead of jumping, Seltzer raised an eyebrow. "That's a good way to get yourself shot."

Jerry started to return the quip when he noticed Seltzer's attire. Jerry had seen him in civilian clothes enough to know the man's summer style generally consisted of shorts and pocketed T-shirts. That being the case, Seltzer looked out of place in khaki slacks and colorful Hawaiian shirt. Of course, if he had been wearing his usual simple attire, the gaudy gold and diamond ring that adorned his perfectly manicured fingers would have seemed out of place.

Jerry glanced at Gunter, who was now sniffing Seltzer's sandaled feet, and rocked back on his heels. "Is that nail polish?"

"Just a glaze—June's idea. She said I had to look like I have money." Seltzer held out his arms. "Jerry, my boy, it's good to see you again."

Jerry stepped into the man's embrace and welcomed several firm pats on the back. "You too, Brian."

"April and Max aren't with you? I was hoping to meet them." The disappointment in Seltzer's voice was evident.

"I didn't want to take a chance of anyone seeing us all together. We'll find a way to get together at some point." Jerry reached into the packet he was holding and handed Brian two phones.

"What's this?"

"Compliments of the agency if you or June need to reach out to me on the cruise."

"What's wrong with our phones?"

"Nothing if you don't mind paying a crazy surcharge for roaming fees. Besides, these will pick up even in the belly of the ship. April added some photos and numbers to make it look legit if anyone else happens to get hold of it. Here are your IDs, and this is the login information to your new social media account," Jerry said, handing over a piece of paper with the information.

Seltzer checked out the documents. "Brian Smith. If that doesn't sound like a made-up name, I don't know what does."

"The agency decided it best to use both your and June's first names and change the last name to something simple, which would pull up enough hits to make the trail a bit more difficult to follow."

"And if the woman is a computer whiz?"

"The agency will be monitoring all communication to and from the ship. If anyone is looking for you or June, they will be directed to what we want them to find." Jerry knew Seltzer would have questions about the legality of this, so he handed him a photo of Bigsby's wife. "This is a current photo of the wife. You and June will be sharing their table in the main dining room, so make sure you are tight on your backstory."

"You seem to be forgetting I was a cop long before you were," Seltzer replied.

"You're a good cop, but you've never worked undercover. Plus, if my spidey senses are right, this woman has already killed at least two people."

"Your spidey senses are never wrong," Seltzer said, eyeing the photo. "She's a looker, but it's a big ship. Any clue how I'm supposed to find her other than dinner?"

"Just keep the phone on. I'll let you know where she is," Jerry told him.

"You're telling me you managed to plant a tracking device? I hate to tell you this, but I think most people would leave personal items in their room."

Jerry nodded to where Gunter stood. "My tracking device is a little more advanced than that."

Seltzer chuckled. "McNeal, if you ever get tired of that dog, send him back to where he belongs."

Gunter lifted his head and looked at Jerry as if waiting for his reply.

"Sorry to disappoint you, sir, but I can assure you that's not going to happen. Gunter is right where he belongs." Jerry glanced at the cab, debating whether to tell his friend about June's visitors. "June seems to be in the zone this morning."

"She is," Seltzer said with a grin. "Had an idea hit her the moment we parked. It sounded good to me, so I told her to do her thing, and I'd wait outside."

Knowing Granny and Bunny were involved, Jerry started to ask about the idea when the passenger side door opened, drawing their attention. June got out and placed a large-brimmed hat on her head. She looked up, saw him, and smiled. Her gaze slid to her husband, and her brow furrowed. "Why didn't you tell me Jerry was here? I swear your mother didn't teach you a lick of manners. If the old bat wasn't dead, I'd phone her up and give her a piece of my mind."

Brian glared at her. "You leave my mother out of this before I bury you next to her!"

Gunter looked at Jerry as if to say, "Are you going to say something or not?"

While Jerry wanted to intervene, he had no clue what to say. As long as he'd known the couple, he'd never heard them as much as raise their voices, much less speak so harshly to each other.

The smile returned, and June moved to the back of the truck. Dressed in a blouse that showed a fair amount of cleavage, she moved close and placed a kiss on Jerry's cheek that lingered just a little too long. "Wowzer, Jerry, you look good enough to eat," she said, pinching him on the backside.

While he'd not seen the woman since leaving Pennsylvania, he didn't recall her ever being this brazen. He remembered Brian telling him about the steamy novels she'd started writing and wondered if that was the reason for the change. Jerry wiped the lipstick from his cheek with his thumb as he took a step back.

"Close your mouth before you swallow a fly." June cackled, the effect distorting her face and turning the normally attractive woman into an unappealing mess.

Jerry suddenly wondered if he'd stepped into the Twilight Zone.

"Gotcha!" June said. She smiled at Brian and softened her tone. "What'd you think?"

"You did great." Seltzer grinned and clapped Jerry on the shoulder. "Boy, you should have seen your face when she grabbed your backside. You looked like a rabbit about to bolt. I'm surprised your spidey senses didn't alert you to this being a ruse."

"I think my spidey senses were as baffled as I

was," Jerry said, relaxing. Actually, the simple fact that his senses hadn't alerted him should have been a giveaway to this having been a farce. He wondered if Bunny and Granny had somehow blocked him from getting a good read on the situation. Regardless of their involvement, any doubts he had about Brian and June being able to pull this off were gone. "June, you missed your calling. You should've been an actress."

"Oh, I plan on making them cast me in the movie role," she replied.

"Movie role?" Jerry looked at Seltzer. "You didn't tell me they're going to make a movie out of June's books."

"They're not. Not yet anyway," June said, answering for him, "but a writer can dream, can't she?"

Seltzer beamed his approval. "They will if they know what's good for them."

And that was the couple he remembered. "It's good to see you two. I'm just sorry I pulled you into this. It sure would be nice just to hang out and catch up."

"Don't you worry about that. I'm aching to meet that new family of yours. I promise we won't let you get away without spending a little time with my new granddaughter." She winked. "I'll have Max calling me Gamma before we return to Pennsylvania."

That June had already claimed the title didn't come as a surprise, as he had always felt she and Brian were more like parents than friends. "I have no doubt that both Max and April will love you as much as I do. Speaking of them, I need to go. I promised I would board the ship with them. Do you need any help with your bags?"

Brian waved him off. "Nope, we got here early and checked in our baggage with the porter before we parked. You go on ahead, June, and I'll be along."

"Roger that, sir."

"McNeal," Seltzer said when Jerry started to walk away. "You look happy. I dare say family life suits you."

"I can honestly say I've never been happier," Jerry said, meaning it.

"Good, don't let her get away."

"Wouldn't dream of it." Jerry nodded to Gunter. "Lead the way, boy."

Chapter Ten

Jerry sat on a lounge chair on the elevated platform overlooking the main pool area. He'd chosen the position as he could easily spy on Lorna and Ted without the couple being the wiser. While he couldn't hear the conversation between Bigsby's widow and Ted, there was a set of stairs that would grant him easy access to the pool area if needed. As an added bonus, Gunter stood at the bottom of the stairs using his energy to stop others from climbing to the upper level. While Jerry could still hear the noise from the pool, the distance allowed him to focus his psychic energy without picking up on everyone in the pool area. Jerry's phone lit up, announcing Seltzer's call.

"Jerry, my boy. I just turned on the mike. Can you hear me?"

"Loud and clear. Lorna and Ted are at the pool. She's wearing a red bikini. You should see them the moment you approach. Just stay to the left and circle until you see the empty lounge chairs beside them."

"And if the chairs aren't empty?"

Jerry looked at the chairs which Granny and Bunny were saving. "Trust me, they'll be empty when you get there."

"We're getting into the elevator now. Wish us luck."

Jerry frowned into the phone. "Why do I suddenly get the feeling there is something you're not telling me?"

The phone crackled. "What's that? I can't hear you. Must be the elevator." The phone went dead.

Gunter woofed.

Jerry watched as Max, Houdini, and his parents moved into the pool area and took position on the opposite side of the pool from Lorna and Ted. A moment later, April came into view. Wearing a yellow sundress and sandals, she carried a tote over her left shoulder. Cupping her right hand over her eyes, she surveyed the pool area and smiled when she spotted him. As she reached the stairs, Gunter moved aside to allow her to pass.

April lowered her bag and slipped the sundress over her head to reveal a yellow bikini. "Anything exciting happening?"

"Not until this minute," Jerry said, looking her over. "Why do I have the sudden desire to remove that with my teeth?"

April laughed a carefree laugh. "And that is why I waited until after you left the cabin to get dressed."

"Come here."

Her laugh turned into a giggle as she moved to

the rail and looked over the pool. "At ease, Marine. We have work to do. I still haven't heard from Mr. Bigsby. Is he here?"

"He's here. He's standing next to his wife."

"Why not sit in one of the two empty chairs?" April turned to face him. "The pool area is almost full. How is it that there just happen to be two empty lounge chairs right next to them?"

"They aren't empty. Granny and Bunny are saving them."

April looked over the rail once more and sighed. Instantly, Jerry knew her disappointment was frustration at not being able to see the spirits. "That trick could come in handy," she said after a moment.

"It can and has served a purpose on more than one occasion," he agreed.

"Speaking of empty chairs," April said. "How is it you managed to get this section all to yourself?"

"Gunter."

"He scared everyone off?"

"He's blocking the way so no one comes up the stairs."

"I came up without any problem."

"That's because he likes you."

"Is his not letting anyone up here his idea or yours?"

"Mine. It helps with the noise level, and I can listen to their conversation without worrying about anyone listening in. The thing is, I don't hear them."

"You think there's a problem?"

"Yes, but not with the microphone. Brian tested

it before getting in the elevator. It worked. It stopped when I called him on the change of plans. I think he turned it off."

"What change of plans?"

"I don't know. I felt it the moment he called, but he disconnected without filling me in."

"He'd better turn it on soon, because they are approaching the pool area," April informed him.

Jerry tried Seltzer's phone. Nothing. He hung up and tried the burner. Still nothing. Jerry stood, searched the pool area and spotted Wayne sitting in a chair. While he had a magazine in his lap, it was doubtful his father was reading it, as the magazine was currently turned upside-down. Houdini sat at his side, intently watching Max, who was in the pool batting a beachball with Lori. While the scene looked innocent enough, Jerry had little doubt that Max was using the game to keep tabs on Lorna and Ted.

Jerry stared at Max, willing her to hear him. *Tell Seltzer his mike isn't working.*

Max threw the beachball too hard and followed it out of the pool. Houdini stood watching as Max passed Seltzer and June as she went to retrieve it. From the look on both their faces, Jerry could tell Max had not only heard him but had successfully relayed the message as she passed, something confirmed when Seltzer reached into his pocket, then cleared his voice.

Jerry heaved a sigh of relief. "Remind me to have the dog bite him."

"Which one?"

"I don't care, as long as it gets done."

"It never ceases to amaze me," April mused.

"What's that?"

"How you and Max are able to communicate like that. It's like you have this invisible bond."

Jerry recalled the time Max was able to read him when he lay frozen in the snow. If not for her, he'd probably be dead. A chill raced up his spine as he remembered the ordeal. He shook it off, focusing on the present.

"They're almost to the chairs," April said. "They'd have made it a bit sooner if June hadn't made Brian carry everything."

"I carry stuff for you all the time," Jerry reminded her.

"Not like that, you don't. The poor guy is loaded like a pack mule. You don't believe me, look."

Jerry stood, walked to the rail and slipped his arm around April's waist. Sure enough, while June was empty-handed, Seltzer carried several bags and a pineapple drink with an orange umbrella. He also carried a pair of sandals that Jerry presumed to be June's, as the woman was wearing high heels.

"Huh," April said.

"Huh, what?"

"From everything you've told me, I thought June and I were more alike. I didn't expect her to be so high maintenance."

Dressed in a flowy coverup, a wide hat, sunglasses, and long red nails, June walked gracefully on her heels, and yet, she was different—extravagant—unlike the motherly woman he'd known for years. While June was normally in shorts and a tank top, the woman before him looked like she'd fit in with the Kardashians. "She's not high maintenance; she's playing the part."

"Hey, Mister?"

Jerry looked to see a boy who looked to be in his early teens standing at the base of the stairs. "Yeah?"

"How'd you get up there?"

"Those stairs." Jerry pointed to where Gunter stood blocking the way.

"They won't let me up. Watch." The boy made several attempts to reach the stairs. Each time, Gunter moved in front of the kid, using some ghostly force to block the boy's way.

Jerry shrugged. "I guess you'd better play someplace else?" He pressed a finger into his earpiece, listening as June instructed Brian on precisely where to set the bags. He was glad he knew this all to be an act; otherwise, he'd feel sorry for the man.

"I don't want to. There's nothing here. Why can't I get up there?" the boy shouted.

"Poor kid," April said. "Maybe you should ask Gunter to let him up."

"There is nothing up here but chairs. That 'poor kid,'" Jerry said, using air quotes, "just wants to get a closer look at you in your bikini."

"He's just a boy," April said.

"A boy in the throes of puberty. If you don't

believe me, watch." Jerry jutted his jaw toward a shapely woman in a microscopic bikini who'd just arrived on the pool deck and was walking straight toward the kid. Sure enough, as her shadow fell over his, the kid turned and trailed after her, losing all interest in climbing the stairs.

"No fair. You're psychic," April said.

Jerry ran his fingers across April's bare back. "Being psychic has nothing to do with it. I was a teenage boy once and know all too well what I would have done in this environment."

"You mean you would have followed her?"

"Nope. I'd have found a way to get up those stairs," Jerry said, moving his hand a bit lower.

"It's go-time," Seltzer whispered into the mike. "Both me and June are live."

"Here we go." Jerry pulled back his hand and returned to the chair where he could watch both couples without being seen, then pulled out a second earpiece and handed it to April so she could listen in.

June moved into the chair just as Bunny vacated then took the drink from Brian. Taking a sip, she puckered her face. "This drink is nothing but water!" she said loud enough to be heard even without her mike.

"It was fine when they made it. You said so yourself," Brian replied.

"I'm telling you, the ice is melted. If you hadn't been so slow, we wouldn't have had this problem."

"I'm sure it's fine," Brian replied. "Drink that one and I'll go get you another."

"Stop patronizing me," June spat. "Just because you're older than I am doesn't give you the right to treat me like a child. If you expect certain privileges tonight, I want another drink, and I want you to bring it to me."

Bunny's voice floated through the device. "Oh, she's good."

"That's Bunny, right?" April asked.

"Yes. I don't know if anyone else is listening, but they do have an audience. Both Bunny and Granny are standing just behind June. Bigsby is standing between Lorna and Ted, and now we have a new spirit."

"Guy or girl?" April asked, craning her neck.

"I don't know. They showed up a few minutes ago and the second spirit hasn't fully materialized. They're standing near Lorna, but I'm not sure if they're connected to Lorna or just watching the show."

"Could it be the first husband?"

"Still no face, but it makes sense," Jerry agreed. "If so, I wouldn't mind having a conversation with him to see what he knows about his death."

"Brian!" June called, waving him back when he was nearly to the other side of the pool.

Brian turned and hurried back to where she lay reclined in the chair. "Yes, love?"

"I'm hungry. Make sure they put extra pineapple in there," she said then waved him away once more.

"I wonder if I should get her to take it down a notch," Jerry said when the couple to June's left began packing up their things.

"No, it's working," April told him.

"How can you tell?"

"Because Lorna stopped scrolling through her phone."

"You can tell that from here?"

"Of course. Before June started in on Brian, Lorna held her phone in her left hand and was using her index finger on her right hand to scroll. She doesn't look like one to read the news, so I figured she is scrolling through social media. That, or the obituaries to find her next victim. Either way, she is much more interested in June and Brian than whatever was on the screen."

"Very good detective work."

"Thanks. I have my moments. Brian's going for the drink. Should we follow him?" April asked.

"Only if Lorna does."

"She won't; she's scrolling again."

Jerry peered at June. "Okay, lady, you have your opportunity. Do something."

Instead of engaging the woman, June took out her cell phone.

Jerry answered her call. "Are you sure this is a good idea?"

"Jerry darling, how's your bod?"

"Is this part of the plan?" Jerry asked when April raised an eyebrow.

"Oh, stop your worrying. You know how much we wanted to take this cruise. If we die, we die. Besides, what's the fun of having all that money if we can't spend it? Please stop. I meant it as a joke. We're not going to keel over, and if either of us does, I'm sure it wouldn't be hard to find someone to comfort whoever is left. Now, don't be like that. I was only teasing. I'm not going anywhere. If you want to worry about anyone, worry about Brian. I've been running him ragged since the ship left port. I know, the doctors advised against this cruise. But they gave us nitro in case there's a problem. Oh, phew, if there's a problem, I call in the chopper. We won't have to wait until we get to port. They can land right here on the ship. That's why we picked this cruise. I know it's expensive, but it isn't like we don't have the money. A person can only spend so much in one lifetime."

"It's working," April said. "She's hanging on every word."

"That's good, June," Jerry said. "You've got her. Now keep it up."

"Stop being a pill. I promise I'm fine. Brian is doing all the heavy lifting. I'll tell you what, stop all this whining and I'll ask Brian to change his will when we get home to leave you enough money to buy yourself an island. Of course I'll do that, and if he doesn't, then I will. I said I would and I will. What would I do with all twenty-seven million?"

April laughed when Ted's head whipped around. "That got both of them."

"Twenty-seven million?" Jerry mused. "Don't you think we could've gone for a million?"

"I know I've come a long way from pushing that

cleaning cart. I just wish I could get the man to dress a little better. He doesn't deserve all that money. I mean, he still drives a pickup truck, for goodness sake! The ring on his finger cost more than that truck." She paused to catch her breath. "I know I bought it for him, but if I was going to be seen with a millionaire, I didn't want him looking like a country bumpkin. Oh, listen, here he comes. I got to go. Wish me luck."

"Good luck." Jerry laughed.

June disconnected the call and reached for her drink as her voice drifted through the listening device. "Did you remember to get extra pineapple?"

"Yes, dear, and plenty of ice." Brian sat on the lounger and swung his feet around.

"Brian darling," June called the moment he relaxed. "I think my blood sugar is low. Perhaps you could get me some cheese and crackers to go with my pineapple. I mean, if it isn't too much trouble."

"No, not too much trouble," Brian replied. "It would have been nice if you'd asked before."

"I didn't want to burden you by making you carry so much," June told him.

"Cheese and crackers. Is there anything else you might need while I am at it?" Brian asked, rising from the chair.

"No, not at all. Cheese and crackers are enough; I wouldn't want to be a bother," June said sweetly.

Brian gave a long look in their direction.

"What's so funny?" April asked when Jerry chuckled.

"I've seen that look a million times," Jerry told her.

"And?"

"It usually precedes the comment, 'Brother, you owe me big time.'"

"Dang," April said as Seltzer walked away.

"Problem?"

"I thought Lorna would follow. You know, swoop in and be the good guy in this all. Instead, she's looking at her phone."

Before Jerry could answer, his cell dinged. "Oh, ye of little faith," he said, showing her the screen.

Chapter Eleven

Jerry stood in the open lobby near the elevator, waiting for Brian and June to arrive for their evening dinner. Though it was his idea to come on the cruise, he'd quickly realized he'd not fully anticipated the noise and energy level of being on a ship designed for fun. As such, he was grateful he knew how to protect himself to dull the energy and had reminded Max to do the same.

Gunter poked his head through the door even before the elevator light clicked off. Pulling it free once more, he eagerly announced Brian and June's arrival as the elevator door slid open, and the couple stepped out. Jerry waved them over.

Gunter, leading the charge, stepped proud as if to say, *Look who I found.*

"Are you sure this is safe?" Seltzer asked.

"Lorna and Ted are already seated."

"April's not with you?" June's voice showed her disappointment.

Seltzer answered for him. "Jerry prefers to work

alone."

Gunter snorted.

Time is ticking. Focus, McNeal. "According to Fred, you two made quite the impression at the pool this afternoon."

Seltzer leaned in closer. "How's that?"

"There were four searches sent out."

Seltzer grinned at June. "Did you hear that, baby? We got four."

"Yep," Jerry agreed. "Two on each of you. The first two searches came while you were still at the pool, and the second was by a different IP address after Ted left. It seems like your little ruse is working, as there were two separate background checks on each of you. I knew you had changed the plan; I just didn't know what you were up to until we realized you'd purposely cast a wide enough net to reel in both Lorna and Ted."

Seltzer shrugged. "You know how those writers are: they're always plotting. June thought it best to dangle a little more bait. Two fish with one pole."

"That's two birds with one stone. Only we aren't talking birds or fish; we are talking about you and June," Jerry said, looking at both in turn. "Do I have to remind you this is not a game?"

Seltzer raised an eyebrow. "You do realize you're talking to the guy who trained you, right?"

"I do. That's why I didn't have any issue bringing you in. June, on the other hand…"

"Is married to a cop," she said, cutting him off. "You know me better than that, Jerry. I am not just some dreamer who sits at the keyboard all day. I know this isn't a game. We both knew what we were getting ourselves into when we signed on. Brian and I trust you. Besides, wouldn't it be better to catch them both? I know Brian always sleeps better when the bad guys are off the street."

"It would," Jerry relented.

Seltzer nodded his agreement. "You said they did a background check. Did they get anything?"

"Only what the agency fed them. The good news is I was able to get the go-ahead to put a bug in their cabin."

Seltzer cocked an eyebrow. "Will this go-ahead stand up in court?"

That Seltzer didn't trust the agency was no secret. "It'll stand up."

"Have you heard anything yet?"

"No. I was just given the okay a few moments ago. I'll head up to their cabin and install the bug before they leave the dining area."

"And if they decide to leave early?"

Jerry nodded to Gunter. "My partner will stall them while I do my thing."

Seltzer followed Jerry's gaze and sighed.

Jerry knew that look all too well, as he'd seen it on multiple occasions when Fred voiced his frustration over not being able to see the dog. Jerry turned his attention to June. "Your little improvisation had the agency scrambling to come up with a reason for all that money. I thought we agreed on a million."

"Size matters." She winked. "Trust me, that woman is smart. If the prize were a million dollars, she'd be interested but take her time. If she thinks she can get her hands on all twenty-seven million, she'll move quickly."

Seltzer laughed. "Tell me your spidey senses aren't telling you she's right."

That was precisely the problem; everything was telling him this would work. The challenge was making sure no one he cared about got hurt in the process. "It'll work."

"You said the agency found a reason for my newfound wealth?"

"Lottery."

"How do you plan on selling that? Don't the states keep records of those things?"

"It's been taken care of." Jerry pulled out his phone and pulled up the fake social media account. Scrolling through, he turned the phone to show a photo of Brian holding a big Pennsylvania lottery check.

Seltzer peered at the phone. "I remember that day. Unfortunately, my bank account doesn't seem to reflect depositing that check."

June nodded her agreement. "That's because you weren't holding a check; you were holding an accommodation for years of service. I know because I was standing right beside you when the picture was taken."

Jerry pocketed the phone. "Photoshop. The story is that Brian won the money, and the two of you got married a short time after. The rest is up to you two."

"Ohh, improv. I love writing on the fly," June replied.

"Come, my little gold-digger." Seltzer offered June his arm. "All that running you made me do today has given me a bear of an appetite."

Jerry slid a glance to June. "Are you actually going to give him a chance to relax and enjoy a meal?"

"I might let him get in a bite or two." June tucked her arm into Seltzer's. "How about it, handsome? Are you ready to have some fun?"

Seltzer patted her hand. "Sweetheart, any day I get to spend with you is a joy."

Gunter yawned and looked at Jerry as if to say, *And I thought you and April were sappy.*

"Listen, I'll go in first. I had the waiter sit them where I can observe their body language while you two are talking," Jerry told them. "Give me a couple of minutes to get settled before you come in. I want to see their faces when they find out you two will be sharing their table."

Having met with his contact on the ship earlier, Jerry had already chosen the McNeal table, opting for one located on a higher tier, which was conveniently positioned just above Seltzer's table. The table sat at an angle that would allow a perfect view without drawing any attention to the fact that they were being watched. While Jerry had chosen a table capable of seating his family, between his father's many trips to the all-you-can-eat ice cream station and Max's discovery of the pizza bar, it meant he would be dining alone this evening. While he hated being away from April and Max, he knew it would be easier to listen to the conversation at the other table without feeling guilty about ignoring the rest of his family. Jerry took a seat and stuck the earpiece in his ear.

Gunter moved to the edge of the elevated platform, crouching to where he had an eagle-eye view of Seltzer's table.

A waiter approached and filled Jerry's water glass. "Good evening, Mr. McNeal. Would you like something to drink, or would you prefer to wait for the rest of your party?"

"Water is fine. I'll be dining alone. I'll have the prime rib dinner with cherry cheesecake for dessert," Jerry said as Brian and June made their way to their table.

"Showtime." Seltzer's words came out in a whisper.

June gasped as she sank into her seat. "Look, honey, it's our neighbors!" Her voice was shrill and verged on yelling.

Seltzer feigned surprise. "Neighbors?"

"From the pool. Don't you remember, they were seated right next to us. I'm telling you, there are no coincidences in this world. The universe brought us together, that's all there is to it. Our getting to know each other was written in the stars!" She stretched her hand over the table. "June Smith, and this is my husband, Brian."

While Lorna merely smiled, Ted took June's hand, holding on just a tad longer than necessary. "It's a delight to meet you. I knew a woman named June once. At the time, I thought her name should have been July, as she was a real firecracker. Now, I'm thinking it might be something in the name."

"The man is a sleaze." Clive Tisdale's spirit took shape in the chair next to Jerry. "Want me to lasso him and toss him off the ship?"

Jerry chuckled as he dug out his Bluetooth and stuck it in his free ear. "No, I think Brian can handle him," he said, keeping his voice low.

"If you change your mind, let me know. I'd be happy to teach that man a thing or two about manners."

"I'd be happy with locking him up for a while." Jerry nodded toward Seltzer, who extended his hand to Ted. "I won't stop you from giving him a hand."

Clive smiled an easy smile and disappeared. The ranger reappeared beside Seltzer and wrapped his hand over Ted's, just as Brian gripped the man's hand.

"I guess my wife and I are going to be your dinner companions during the cruise," Seltzer told him.

Given the pinched look on Ted's face, Jerry knew Clive had administered a strong handshake.

Seltzer released the man's hand and extended his to Lorna.

"Why, Mr. Smith." Lorna's voice was silky soft. "That is some ring. It's almost as large as the one your wife is wearing."

June held her arm out, studying the ring on her finger. "I could give you the name of my jeweler if you'd like. Unless your husband doesn't have as much money as mine, then it would just make you depressed."

Jerry laughed, then covered it with a cough.

"He's not my husband." Lorna's tone let them know June had hit a nerve.

"Lorna and I are just friends." Even though Lorna started it, the comment must have infuriated her, as the woman's face turned a brilliant shade of pink. She recovered just as quickly and turned her attention back to Brian. "I must ask if it's real."

"It's real," June answered for him. "I should know, I wrote the check myself."

"With my money," Seltzer mumbled under his breath.

Jerry noted the way Lorna's lip curved, and nodded his approval.

"Your wife has great taste. Tell me, Brian, what do you do for a living?" Lorna asked.

Before Seltzer could answer, their waiter approached the table, taking their order. "I'm retired," he said when the man walked away.

"From? I'm just asking, as it sounds as if it was a very important job," Lorna cooed.

"Radios," Seltzer replied.

Lorna's face lit up. "You were on the radio?"

June laughed. "Have you heard him speak? Of course he wasn't on the radio; he fixed the things."

June glanced at Seltzer. "Sorry, old man, but we both know your talents lie elsewhere."

"You mean?" Seltzer started.

"Don't flatter yourself, honey. You're nothing without that little blue pill. I'm talking about your ability to pick the winning lottery numbers."

Ouch, Jerry thought, feeling the jab. *If I didn't know the whole thing to be a ruse, I'd think June to be a real...*

"Your meal, sir," the waiter said, placing a plate in front of him.

Jerry removed the Bluetooth earpiece but left the small listening device in place.

"My manager said you asked for the visits to your table to be as brief as possible. I trust you'll let me know if you require anything."

Jerry looked over his plate. "I will. Everything looks good. Thank you." He waited for the man to leave then tapped his earpiece to increase the volume. While he'd missed their initial responses, obviously June had succeeded in hooking both fish, who now sat leaning in, listening to her weave her tale.

June rubbed at her arms. "I don't know why they insist on keeping this room so cold. Brian, darling, do be a dear and fetch my shawl."

"But we haven't ordered yet."

"I am perfectly capable of ordering for you," June told him.

"Yes, dear." Seltzer pushed his chair back and left without another word.

"Did you two know each other before he won the money?" Lorna asked after he'd gone.

"Nope. I met Brian in the ER when he had his first heart attack."

Lorna blinked in surprise. "You're a nurse?"

"Heavens no, I don't do with all those needles. I was working as a janitor. There I was mopping the floor, when I pulled back the curtain and saw my Brian."

"Love at first sight, was it?" Ted asked.

June cackled, and the dining room grew quiet. She lowered her voice. "Sorry, but I was just picturing him the first time I saw him. She puffed her cheeks before she spoke. "The man was a puffer fish. Bloated to all get out. I tiptoed in, aiming to mop around his bed, and that's when I recognized him."

"So, you did know him," Lorna said.

"No, but I'd seen his picture on the television saying as how he'd won a bunch of money. They'd done this whole story on him, and I knew he wasn't married, and I thought, 'Martha June, here's your chance. All you have to do is be nice to him and he'll give you some of that money.' It was a good thing he did, on account of later I found out he didn't have any kids or anyone else to share it with. Heaven knows where that money would have gone if something had happened to him before he married me."

"I'm afraid I don't see it," Lorna replied.

"You don't see what?"

"Seems to me the opposite is true."

"I'm still not reading you."

"The man has a heart condition, and you're running him ragged. You're not afraid he'll die?"

"Oh, dear." June's voice trembled as she spoke. "I'm afraid you've read me all wrong. I'm not trying to kill the man; I'm just trying to survive. The truth of the matter is, while my husband's heart is bad, it is in much better shape than mine."

"And that right there is the zinger," Clive said, returning to Jerry's table.

"And what if something happened to you both?" Lorna asked.

"Well, I have a sister; that's who I was talking to on the phone earlier. She worries about me. The rest will probably go to a charity or something. I guess we haven't given that any thought. How sweet of you to ask. You're right, though, I guess we'll have to get that figured out as soon as we get back home." June picked up her cellphone and spoke into it. "Note, call Mr. Felps as soon as we return to Florida and see if he can get us in ASAP to draw up a new will."

Jerry stopped chewing mid-bite as the hair on the nape of his neck prickled. A second later, his cell phone buzzed with a message from Fred. > *Get that bug planted.*

Jerry pocketed his phone and glanced at Clive. "I need to get into a locked stateroom. Can you help me?"

"Yep."

Jerry raised his hand to get the waiter's attention.

"Which one do you think will give you what you need?"

Jerry smiled a confident smile. "With a little luck, the bug will allow us to catch them both."

Chapter Twelve

The lobby outside the restaurant was full of passengers. Some were waiting for one of the six elevators, while others mingled waiting for the rest of their party. Knowing Fred had ears on Seltzer and June, Jerry removed his earpiece and took the stairs two at a time as Gunter raced ahead of him. Jerry didn't stop to question whether the dog was heading the right way; it was Gunter. The ghostly K-9 was never wrong.

A cruise attendant rounded a passageway, pushing a cart full of towels. The man looked like he was in his early twenties and appeared to be in no big hurry as he made his way down the long hallway, listening to whatever was playing on the earbuds protruding from his ears. Seeing how odd the man looked with them sticking out of his ears made Jerry glad he'd removed his ancient Bluetooth earbud before leaving the table.

He slowed his pace, nodding a greeting as he passed, then continued down the long hallway, pausing when Gunter stopped and stuck his head through the door to a stateroom and wagged his tail. As the dog pulled his head free, the door clicked open.

At first, Jerry thought Gunter had opened the door, a thought he quickly rejected at seeing Clive standing in the middle of the room. The second thing that caught his attention was the fact there were two beds in the room. "Looks like that Bigsby fellow was telling the truth."

"How's that?" Clive asked.

"About Lorna refusing to sleep with her husband before marriage."

Clive looked at the beds. "Seems like that Ted fellow might be more of a gentleman than I gave him credit for."

Jerry pulled the bug from his pocket, small and cream-colored. It was easy to tell why they'd selected this particular device, as it was designed to blend in with the painted rivets that lined the walls. He activated it and showed it to Clive.

The ranger lifted his head and looked down his nose at the device. "Doesn't look like any bug I've ever seen."

"It's a listening device," Jerry clarified. "This piece gets planted in the room and then we can listen in on their conversation."

"There's no dirt."

"Dirt?"

Clive waved a finger toward the device. "For the planting."

"It's not that kind of planting." Jerry hid a smile as he looked about the room for the best place to plant the bug so it would hear any conversation in the small stateroom. That the couple hadn't opted for a balcony room was a plus, not that he thought either party dense enough to devise a plan where they could be overheard. Nor was he worried about the bathroom, as the space was barely large enough for one person. He decided to hedge his bet; splitting the difference between the sleeping area and the small sofa, he stuck the device to the wall. That Fred had known the exact color of the wall amazed him. Then again, it was Fred, the man had access to things most mere mortals could only dream of. He moved to the far wall. "Testing. Testing, can you hear me?"

"Of course I can hear you. I'm standing right here," Clive replied.

Jerry's phone chimed with a message from Fred. > *Loud and clear, even before you asked. Barney and I are taking bets on who you're talking to.*

"What are the choices?" Jerry asked.

"Choices for what?" Clive asked.

"My boss is trying to figure out who I am talking to."

Clive took three steps and peered at the wall. "So that thing really works?"

Jerry's phone chimed. "Barney is convinced I'm talking to my grandmother. Fred's money is on Bunny."

"Your boss thinks you talk to rabbits?" Clive's voice was incredulous. "Who does that?"

Jerry started to tell him that most people would say the same about his talking to spirits but decided against it. "Not bunny rabbits. Bunny, the spirit with the pink hair." He told Fred, "You both get to keep your money, and thanks for not suggesting a psych exam."

Gunter barked, and both he and Clive disappeared.

"Anything happening that I need to know about?" Jerry asked then waited for the text.

Fred > *June's still laying it on thick, but they just got served dessert, so it shouldn't be too much longer.*

Good, but not reassuring. Jerry sent a text to April as he left the cabin. > *Everything good?*

>*Yes, all good here,* she wrote back. *Max is at the pool with your mom, and if I had to guess, I would say your dad is making his 17th trip to the ice cream bar. Seriously, that man needs an intervention.*

> *Sounds like my dad. The bug is in place. I'm on my way back*, Jerry replied. He smiled when April answered with a single heart for him and a paw print for Gunter, who had yet to return, but could very well have left to join his father at the ice cream bar.

***

Jerry sat on the small couch with April, waiting. According to a text from Seltzer, he and June had followed Lorna and Ted into the elevator and watched the couple get off at their assigned floor.

"You're tense," April said, rubbing his neck. "Do

you have a bad feeling?"

"No." The truth of the matter was that, despite having his whole family involved, he was feeling pretty good about things. "I just want this to be over. It's your first cruise, and we've barely seen each other. I was sitting at dinner watching all those couples, and I missed you."

"I missed you too."

"No, I mean I really missed you. I want to marry you."

"Yes, I know." April waved her hand in front of his face. "That's why you gave me this ring."

"Now."

April's forehead furrowed. "Now?"

"Well, not this minute, but on the ship. I want the captain to marry us."

"Did something happen today that you're not telling me about?"

"It's not just about one thing. It's about…"

There was a knock on the cabin door.

April hurried to answer and moved aside to allow Brian and June to enter. From the perspiration on their brows, it looked as if they'd been running.

Jerry moved to the edge of the bed to allow them to take the couch. "Take it easy, old man, or you might just have that heart attack after all."

"I can outrun you any day," Seltzer quipped. "April Buchanan, it is a delight to finally meet you. I'd hug you, but…"

"Oh no you don't. You're not getting by without a proper hug." April wrapped her arms around the man, then did the same to June. "Jerry has told me so much about you both."

"She's even more beautiful in person." June waited for April to turn away and hoisted her thumb in the air, giving Jerry a thumbs-up to show her approval.

Seltzer nodded to the listening device. "Hear anything yet?"

"They haven't made it to their room yet."

Seltzer and June exchanged glances. "They left at the same time we did. I thought they'd have been back by now."

The room grew quiet when a loud bang sounded through the listening device.

"You're going to have to talk to me at some point," Ted's voice said, drifting through the device.

"What was all that about?!" Lorna replied.

"What was what?"

"You told that shrew we aren't married."

"Who's she calling a shrew?" April asked, then giggled as both Jerry and Seltzer pointed to June.

"We're not married," Ted reminded her.

"It's the way you said it," Lorna snapped. "Why were you all over the old hag?"

"I don't think she likes me very much. And I'm not that much older than her. Not a word," June said when Seltzer opened his mouth to respond.

"For the same reason you were buttering up the old guy. Money."

"It's called conversation. You should try it."

"You were practically drooling over him ever

since you laid eyes on that ring he was wearing."

"It's bigger than the one you got me."

"Her tone is changing," June pointed out. "They're either about to, you know, or she's forming a plan."

"It has to be a plan," April told her. "She has rules."

"There were two beds in the room," Jerry agreed.

"The man has some willpower," Seltzer said under his breath.

"You just make sure you have the same if she comes up to you or I'll stick that ring…"

Jerry cleared his throat.

"I was going to say back in the box and straight back to the store," June said innocently.

Gunter lifted his head and looked at Jerry as if to say, *If you believe that, I have some land to sell on the other side.*

"Focus, everyone. We don't want to miss anything."

"You know, I could get it for you," Ted said after a moment.

"You want to buy me that ring?"

"Who said anything about buying it?"

"You're planning on stealing it?" Instead of being surprised, Lorna sounded intrigued.

"The guy's worth twenty-seven mil; it's not like he'd miss it."

"He wouldn't miss it if he were dead," Lorna said.

"I think you're forgetting the fact that he's

married."

"To a woman with a bad heart." Lorna's voice was cold and calculated. "I see the books you read. You're telling me you'd have qualms about killing her?"

"There's a difference in reading about murder and doing the deed," Ted said dryly.

"Okay, it was a silly fantasy anyway." Lorna's voice was lighter now.

"Just to keep things interesting," Ted said, "tell me how you'd do it."

"We," Lorna replied. "This only works if we decide to do it together."

"I'm listening."

"We kill the wife, and then I swoop in, being the epitome of concern to help the man through his grief. Once I gain his trust, I get him to make a will, leaving it all to me."

Jerry watched as Brian placed a protective hand on June's knee.

"Where is the 'we' in that?" Ted asked.

"You and I get together afterwards. It won't raise suspicion, as we are already together. It will just look like we've kissed and made up. The only thing we need to figure out is how to do it. Her heart is bad, so it shouldn't be that difficult."

"I don't like it."

"What don't you like?"

"I don't like the thought of you sleeping with the guy when you haven't even slept with me."

"Don't be silly. We've slept together every

night."

"That's the problem: we sleep. You and your rules. You're going to tell me you'd make him wait?"

"Sweetheart, for a chance at twenty-seven million, I'd do just about anything." Lorna laughed a carefree laugh. "Heck, I've done far worse for less."

Jerry felt a tingle at the back of his neck as Mr. Bigsby appeared in the room. "Here it comes."

"How much worse?"

"Let's just say I know how to kill a man and not get caught."

"Come on, darling, tell us how you did it," Jerry encouraged.

"You just said you have to figure out how."

"Yes, because it is a woman."

"What's the difference?"

"She doesn't take Viagra."

"I'm not following you."

"You can't take Viagra and nitroglycerin together. The combination can be catastrophic."

Jerry looked at Bigsby. "Did you take both?"

"No, just the Viagra. Lorna wasn't even there. She knew I'd be home soon and so she called and reminded me." He shrugged. "They need time to work."

"How'd you take them?"

"It's a pill. I took it with lemonade from my thermos. And before you ask, I didn't put a nitro tablet under my tongue."

"Who's he talking to?" June asked.

"Mr. Bigsby," April told her.

"Is that how you killed your husband?"

"Husbands, plural."

"They didn't do an autopsy?"

"I didn't request one. It was the perfect setup. I put the nitro tablets in their thermos and then waited. For my last husband, I waited until close to lunchtime. I called and told him I left one of my undergarments in his lunch box, and if he came home early, I would …you get the picture. I reminded them to take their pill, knowing they would use the thermos to wash it down. It was the perfect murder, and I was able to swoop in and play the distraught widow."

"You told me you've been married twice. No one questioned both husbands dying the same way?"

"No one knew. I moved and made all new friends whom I cultivated very carefully. They all knew how much I loved my husband and how concerned I was about their heart issues. I even fixed them a healthy lunch each day and made sure they had fresh-squeezed lemonade that would mask anything out of the ordinary. I was never around at the time of death. My first husband was at the gym. I knew he would opt to swim a few laps before heading home, and there were plenty of witnesses in the pool, so neither one was disputed. And if you're thinking of telling anyone, both of my husbands were cremated, so it will be your word against mine. So tell me, are you in or are you out?"

"I'm in. Just tell me what I need to do," Ted told her. "But you have to promise to marry me when all is said and done."

"You still want to marry me after what I told you? Aren't you afraid I'll… you know."

"You've been offing old men for their money. We pull off this deal and you'll have more money than you and I can spend in a lifetime. But just so you know, I'm never drinking any of your lemonade."

Seltzer slapped his knee. "That's it. We've got them both on conspiracy to commit murder."

"Okay, tell me I'm not the only one who just got a chill," April whispered.

June rubbed at her arms. "Nope, not the only one."

Bigsby sank onto the bed with a heavy sigh. "I guess you were right."

"I'm sorry," Jerry told him. "Maybe now, you'll be able to move on."

"Lorna keeps a diary," Bigsby said.

"You mean she writes everything down?"

"For as long as I've known her, writes in it every night. Paul—that was her first husband—told me she kept one with him as well. I suspect if you give her a few hours, you'll have what you need."

Jerry was incredulous. "You know, if you'd led with that, we could have gotten a warrant to search her apartment."

"I didn't know until Paul showed up by the pool and reminded me. Even if I had, it wouldn't have changed anything. The guy she's dating is a fraud."

Jerry laughed, but the humor didn't reach his eyes. "I'm pretty sure she knows that, or she wouldn't have enlisted him in her little scheme."

Bigsby nodded his agreement.

"I'm sorry," Jerry said once more.

"She was good to me."

"Until she killed you," Jerry reminded him.

"There's that," Bigsby agreed. He nodded to April. "You trust that one?"

Jerry smiled. "She hasn't given me a reason not to."

"The husband is usually the last to know." With that last statement, Bigsby vanished.

"He's gone," Jerry said when Bigsby disappeared.

Seltzer stood and clapped Jerry on the back. "Jerry, my boy, I want to be you in my next life."

"Oooh," June said, joining him. "Think of all the fodder I could get for my novels. It could be a whole ghostly series."

Jerry chuckled. "You've said that before. I'm not sure anyone would be interested in my life."

"Don't sell yourself short, Jerry." June gave him a peck on the cheek. "You're a good man. Add in that ghost dog of yours, and the possibilities would be endless."

"So, what's next?" Seltzer asked. "We going to put them in the brig?"

"Bigsby said the woman keeps a journal that she writes in every night. While the recording should be sufficient to nail them both with conspiracy to commit murder, I say we let her put her thoughts into words. In the meantime, neither of you are to have any more communication with either of them," Jerry said as Clive and Gunter returned to the room.

"Is that your spidey senses talking? You think they'll try something tonight?"

Clive took off his hat, ran his hands through his hair, then settled it on his head once more. "Don't you worry about those two scoundrels. I'll keep an eye on them for you."

Jerry shook his head. "No, I think this is over."

Brian wrapped an arm around June. "Come, my dear, I'll buy you an ice cream."

Gunter looked at Jerry and licked his lips.

"What's so funny?" Seltzer asked when Jerry laughed.

Jerry nodded to Gunter, who now stood staring at the cabin door. "Looks like you two are getting a police escort."

Seltzer glanced at the door. "Gunter?"

"Yep."

The man grinned. "I knew that dog liked me."

Jerry started to tell his friend it was the promise of ice cream that had motivated the dog but decided to allow him this small victory. It was the least he could do after all Brian and June had done to help get Bigsby's wife to confess.

"Where were we?" Jerry asked when he and April were alone.

"You started to tell me something earlier. You asked me to marry you but said it wasn't about just one thing."

"It's not. I don't care if we are together or I'm away on a job, I want to go to bed each night knowing you're my wife. I want to formally adopt Max and go on vacation wearing matching shirts that say Team McNeal and know that, above all, we share two things: love and the same last name."

April laughed. "You want to marry me and adopt my daughter so we can wear matching shirts?"

"That, and the fact that I love your detective skills."

April feigned surprise. "You're saying you're not marrying me for my money?"

"Nope, I mean, I've seen the offer Fred sent over, and it is a lot of money, but not so much that I plan on killing you off to get my hands on it. How about you? I must ask, are you marrying me for my money?"

April shook her head. "Nope. I've got my own."

"So, I guess that means you really do love me."

April giggled. "That, and I have no intention of giving you a reason to come back and haunt me."

"Oh, you don't have to worry about giving me a reason. Haunting you is a given," Jerry said, pulling her into his arms.

Chapter Thirteen

Jerry returned to the cabin just as the in-cabin speaker crackled.

Gunter tilted his head, listening as the cruise director started speaking.

"Attention, all passengers, please clear the upper deck for an inbound helicopter that will be evacuating a medical emergency. I repeat, please clear the upper deck for an inbound helicopter."

"Well, that's creative," April said when the speaker quieted.

Jerry chuckled. "The captain thought it would be better than letting the ship's passengers know they've been cavorting with murderers."

"Murderer. Technically, Ted was only conspiring to kill someone," April reminded him. "How did Lorna and Ted handle being arrested?"

"As well as could be expected. Both denied everything at first, then Ted threw her under the bus and confessed to everything we already knew."

"So I guess that wedding is off?"

"Unless they plan on a virtual wedding from the prison, I think that's a safe guess," Jerry told her. "Speaking of weddings, I spoke with the captain, who said he'd be thrilled to perform our ceremony tomorrow afternoon at 3:00 if that's okay with you."

"Okay."

"You don't sound so sure."

"I just want to make sure I can get a spa appointment before the wedding."

"I knew you'd say that, which is why it is already booked. I hope you don't mind. I took the liberty of booking it the moment I got the okay from the captain. I set up for half spa day appointments for you, Mom and Max, starting at 10. Massage, manicure and pedicure, and hair. Are you sure you're okay getting married without a wedding dress? I would love to marry you, but I don't want you to look back at the photos and have any regrets."

"I'm good. I'll wear the dress I brought for formal night."

"The one you bought while shopping with my mother and wouldn't let me see?"

April smiled a brilliant smile. "That's the one. Isn't it a good thing I didn't let you see it?"

"You don't believe in all that 'don't see the groom before the wedding day' nonsense, do you?"

"My last marriage didn't turn out so well," April said softly. "I think maybe I'll opt for tradition this time."

Jerry felt instant regret for having pushed for an unconventional marriage.

"I'm sorry. I guess it's poor taste to mention my ex when we are going to be married tomorrow."

"I'm not worried about Randy. It's just that I was thinking about what I want and …"

April reached a finger to his lips. "Stop, I'm fine with getting married on the ship."

Gunter woofed. Jumping off the bed, he went to the door and stuck his head through, removing it as someone knocked.

"It's Max."

"How did you…oh."

"Hazard of the job," Jerry said, opening the door.

Max stepped inside. Houdini raced ahead of her, whining a greeting to Gunter, the two prancing around the room as if it'd been years since last seeing each other.

"What's a hazard of the job?" Max asked.

"Knowing it was you before I opened the door. I also know you're ticked off about something, so out with it?"

"It's Grandma."

Jerry glanced at April. "What did my mother do?"

"She's treating me like a baby. I told her I was going to go meet the helicopter, and she told me I couldn't on account of there's a medical emergency. Only there's not. Uncle Fred's coming in and doesn't want anyone to know it."

Jerry frowned. "Uncle Fred's not coming; he's sending his helicopter to pick up our prisoners."

Max firmed her chin. "He's coming. He told me

so himself."

"When did you talk to him?"

"Last night. I had to tell him about the wedding."

Jerry glanced at April. "I thought we were going to tell her together."

April shook her head. "I didn't say a word."

"Mom didn't tell me. I just knew."

"Okay, I get that. But why did you tell Uncle Fred?" Jerry asked.

"Because I promised him I would."

"When?"

Max shrugged. "Months ago, when you first asked Mom to marry you. Uncle Fred told me you and Mom might sneak away to get married, and he made me promise to tell him as soon as I found out."

"Did Uncle Fred tell you why?"

"Sure. He said weddings are important and that Mom needed someone she could trust."

"Trust to do what, Max?" April asked.

Max grinned. "Walk you down the aisle. He said since you don't have a dad, you can count on him to be your stand-in dad. Kind of like he's my stand-in uncle."

"Did you know about this?" April asked, wiping at a string of tears.

"No, but it doesn't surprise me," Jerry replied. "The man has had a soft spot for you and Max even before he met you."

Max brightened. "Does that mean you'll talk to Grandma Lori and tell her I can go meet the helicopter?"

"Yes, I'll talk to your grandmother," Jerry promised.

"Maybe Mom can keep her company while we are waiting for the helicopter," Max suggested.

April frowned. "I don't get to watch the helicopter?"

"Nope, you and my mother have an appointment with the pastry chef to discuss wedding cakes. I don't care what flavor, as long as it's chocolate." Okay, he'd not actually set up the meeting, but the man had promised to make a cake.

April laughed. "And your mother is involved why?"

Jerry waggled his eyebrows. "Because it will keep her from smothering Max and fussing at Dad, who is probably at the ice cream bar even as we speak."

Another laugh. "Meaning you want me to take one for the team."

"Do you mind?"

"No, I love Lori. Maybe if I had a mother who cared as much as she does, my life would have turned out differently." April must have realized what she'd said as her face turned crimson. "Oh, Max, I didn't mean..."

Max shrugged off the comment. "I know, Mom. I wish things had been different too, but if they had, maybe we wouldn't have met Jerry and Gunter."

April wrapped her arms around Max. "You are one smart girl."

Max grinned. "I know."

April opened her arms. "Come on, Jerry, group hug."

Jerry walked into their embrace, everyone laughing as both Gunter and Houdini rose onto their hind legs to join in.

***

Jerry wasn't sure what Max was hiding, but he knew the girl was holding back. This was made clear when she hadn't wanted her mom to join them to watch the helo. He was just getting ready to ask her what it was when Seltzer joined them in the hallway.

"Hey, kiddo," Seltzer said upon seeing Max.

Max giggled. "That's what Jerry calls me, only I'm not a kid."

"I could call you Maxine," Seltzer teased.

"Max is fine."

"Max it is." His gaze trailed to Houdini. "Boy, if that dog isn't the spitting image of his father."

Max gaped at Jerry. "You told him?"

"I did."

"You said it's not safe to tell anyone." There was a bite to her tone.

"I told Brian because he's my friend."

"So, Chloe is my friend and you said I couldn't tell her."

Jerry motioned her forward. "Talk while we walk. We have to get to the helo pad."

"It doesn't seem fair. Mom got to tell Carrie because she's her best friend, and you told Mr. Seltzer because he's your best friend. I should be able to tell my best friend."

"Maybe someday. But not yet. We've been through this before. Friends change. Friends we have as kids aren't always the same ones we have as adults. If Chloe gets mad at you, she might retaliate by telling all your secrets. People find out, and it could put Houdini in danger. I know it doesn't seem possible right now, but trust me, life has a way of tossing you curveballs when you least expect it."

"If it helps, I can attest to that fact," Seltzer said. "I even know some adults I wouldn't trust to keep secrets."

"Fine. I won't tell her." Max took the lead with Gunter and Houdini by her side.

"She seems to be a good kid," Seltzer said.

"I heard that. I'm not a kid."

"Max," Jerry cautioned.

"Well, I'm not."

"I'll tell you what, I'll stop calling you a kid if you stop calling me Mr. Seltzer."

Max turned to face them and continued walking backwards. "Then what do I call you?"

"Oh, I don't know. Grampa, Grandad, Pops. Pop Pop. You pick it."

"Okay." Max turned and walked forward once more, stopping when they reached the elevator. "I have a Grandpa Wayne. I don't think he'd like it if I call you Grandpa Brian. Jerry calls him Pops, so I don't think that would be right either. What about Pappy? That's what Chloe calls her grandpa."

"Perfect," Seltzer said as the elevator slid open. He stepped aside to allow them to enter, then released the door and pushed the button for the upper deck. "I'm a Navy man. Pappy suits me just fine. Now you'll need to find a name for June. Make it a good one, on account of that woman plans to spoil you rotten."

Max pulled her phone out of her pocket. "I'll text Chloe to ask what she calls her grandmother."

The elevator came to a stop, and both dogs turned to face the door. As it slid open once more, they were greeted by a cruise ship employee. The man held up his hand to prevent them from exiting. "Sorry, folks. The deck is closed for an incoming helicopter. It will reopen once the helo departs."

Jerry flashed his badge. "The captain is expecting us."

The guy moved aside to allow them to pass.

Seltzer gave a nod to where the captain was chatting with some of the crew. "I'm going to talk with the captain and see if I can get an ETA on the chopper."

"Okay, spill it," Jerry said when Seltzer was out of earshot.

Max feigned innocence. "What?"

"Why didn't you want your mother to come?"

"Because she would have ruined the surprise."

"You already told her Fred was coming," Jerry reminded her. "What else is going on?"

Max sighed. "Uncle Fred's not the only one coming. He's bringing Carrie."

"Carrie?"

"Mom's friend."

Jerry resisted rolling his eyes. "I know who Carrie is. Why is she coming?"

"Because you can't have a wedding without a maid of honor."

Jerry was impressed. "And was this your idea or Uncle Fred's?"

"Neither. Bunny suggested it."

"Bunny?" Unexpected, but nice all the same.

"Yep, she thought it would make Mom happy, so I asked Uncle Fred what he thought. He said he thought it was a grand idea and promised to make it happen. I like Uncle Fred; he's one of the good guys."

Fred Jefferies was an enigma that Jerry had always held at a distance as he'd questioned the man's motives on more than one occasion. That Max didn't share his reservations gave Jerry hope that Fred was the real deal. "Yes, Max. I believe he is."

"They're coming," Max said as Brian joined them once more.

Gunter sniffed the air and woofed his agreement.

Brian cupped his hand over his eyes, looking out at the sea. "The captain said it wouldn't be long, but I don't see anything."

Jerry smiled. "Neither does she, but she's right."

"You can feel it?"

"Max zeroed in on it before I did," Jerry admitted. "But I do now. It should be coming into view any moment."

A moment later, Max thrust her hand toward the sky. "There it is. Oooh, it's orange."

"Looks to be Coast Guard," Jerry told her.

"Probably coming out of Gitmo," Seltzer agreed.

"Max, take Houdini to the back rail until they land. Those blades are pretty powerful and we don't want to chance any debris getting into his eyes."

"Okay, Jerry." Max clapped the side of her leg and jogged away with Houdini at her side.

"She's a good kid," Seltzer said for the second time.

"The best," Jerry agreed. "Any plans for tomorrow afternoon?"

"Eating too much and chilling by the pool."

"April and I are getting married at three. We'd love for you to join us."

Brian's face lit up like a candle. "Jerry, my boy, you know June and I wouldn't miss it for the world. Seriously, that is just outstanding news. I should call June. I'll never hear the end of it if she's the last to know."

Jerry braced against the wind as the helicopter hovered over the helo pad and eased its way down without incident. The helo powered down and the door opened even before the blades stopped spinning. Fred Jefferies coolly stepped out. Wearing a dark suit and even darker shades, the man was the epitome of every men in black scenario, real or imagined. He saw Jerry and cracked the slightest of smiles. Once off the helicopter, he turned and held his hand out to Carrie. To his surprise, Carter followed her out then reached in to retrieve several suitcases. Behind him was the same shadowy spirit that was attached to the man when they'd met in Frankenmuth. He hadn't told him of the haunting then and wondered if he should make the time to speak with the spirit to see if there was a reason he was haunting the man.

"McNeal," Fred said, drawing his attention. "I've come bearing gifts."

Looking like a woman who'd just had the thrill of a lifetime, Carrie's face was flushed, her eyes twinkling as she looked around, presumably for April. Not seeing her, she turned her attention to Jerry. "So, you two are finally doing this?"

Jerry smiled. "We are."

"It's about dang time," she said and hugged him furiously. "Where is she? I'm sure she is beside herself trying to get ready."

Houdini's barks filled the air. Jerry turned to see Max and the dog running to greet them.

Carrie hugged Max then knelt to greet the dog, who wiggled into her lap and smothered her with K-9 kisses.

Gunter snorted. Jerry dropped his hand to the ghostly K-9's head to keep him from feeling left out.

"Max, can you take Carrie to see your mom?"

"Sure," Max said, bobbing her head.

"I'll have someone deliver your luggage to your stateroom," Fred said when the woman hesitated.

"I don't know how you pulled this off, but April is going to be thrilled," Jerry told him after Carrie and Max left.

"It was easy," Fred said. "I promised her a trip to

Cuba, a ride on a helicopter and a cruise to Mexico in a private cabin."

"I can see where that would have its draws." Jerry glanced at Carter, who was talking to Seltzer. "What's he doing here?"

"Carter and Agent Hoover will be escorting the prisoners. Agent Hoover is still on the chopper. She'll be escorting Mrs. Bigsby, unless you wish to do the honors, but a little bird told me you have other plans."

"Yes, Max made a full confession about spilling the beans," Jerry informed him. "She said you are planning on giving April away. Does that mean you'll be staying on the ship?"

"I'm paying for the rooms, so I may as well use one of them."

"I'm not following you."

"You recall there were no rooms to be had when we first tried to get you on?"

"Yes. Then the wedding party canceled at the last minute."

"The cruise line balked at booking new passengers at the last moment, so we sweetened the deal by claiming all the rooms and agreeing to personally vet who uses them."

Jerry raised an eyebrow. "How many rooms?"

"Ten in total, so let me know if you want to invite anyone else to the wedding. I'm sure Carter would love a return trip."

"I think we're good."

"You don't like the man very much, do you?"

Jerry considered this for a moment. It wasn't that he had anything against the man, but seeing him had brought back the memory of his making a fool of himself in Frankenmuth when he'd heard the thunder snow. Add to that the guy was uber arrogant, and he just seemed to rub him the wrong way. "I don't know the man well enough to have an opinion of him," Jerry said as Clive Tisdale appeared.

"You talking about that young feller who got off that whirly bird?" Clive asked. "The man's a pretty boy. We used to call his type a rooster strutting around like he's looking for a hen to conquer or someone to fight."

"What's so funny?" Fred asked when Jerry smiled.

Jerry repeated what Clive had said.

Fred's eyes grew wide. "That spirit's here now?"

Jerry gave a nod to where Clive stood.

"Riddle me this," Fred said, looking at where Jerry had indicated. "How is it spirits can leave things behind?"

"I'm not following you, boss."

"We got an alert on your vehicle."

The hairs on the back of Jerry's neck tickled. "Someone messed with the Durango?"

"A young man snuck into the parking garage doing some smash and goes. Several cars were vandalized before he zeroed in on your ride. Now, if you watch the video, it would appear that boy met up with a swarm of bees as he was yelling and screaming and running every which way with no apparent cause. He ran around that SUV three times before becoming perfectly still and walking away at a fast clip with his arms glued to his side. Instead of leaving, he stayed in that same position, his face frozen in terror as he weaved in and around each row. By the time the local PD arrived, the young man was gone, but the officers claim to have seen several piles of fresh horse manure."

Jerry looked at Clive. "This was the thing you had to take care of?"

Clive motioned to Gunter, who smiled a K-9 smile. "The dog did most the chasing; I did the capturing. Got that lasso on nice and tight and walked him in and around each and every one of those automobiles. I didn't hurt the fellow, but I believe he'll think twice before vandalizing cars."

Jerry relayed what Clive said and watched Fred's face with the telling. While Fred hadn't seen the spirits, having seen the video, it was apparent he could now clearly picture the events as they unfolded.

Chapter Fourteen

Unable to sleep, Jerry made his way to the upper deck and sat looking up at the blanket of stars. Gunter dropped to the deck near his chair, sprawling out under the glow of the moonlight. Stars, too many to count, filled the night sky. Many times during his deployments with the Marines, he'd snuck up to the flight deck in the wee hours of the night and lay on the steel beach, looking at stars and wishing he'd had someone special to share it with. While he wanted nothing more than to call April and ask her to come share it with him, he knew what her answer would be, as she'd insisted on spending the night in Carrie's cabin so they wouldn't see each other until time to say their vows. Tomorrow, he told himself, they would sit beneath the stairs and share them for the first time as husband and wife.

As Jerry surveyed the sky, picking out constellations, he thought about how much his life had changed over the last year. He'd gone from running from his gift to embracing it, and in the process had found a family to keep him grounded. He took in a long breath and blew it out slowly, feeling a sense of deep satisfaction in knowing that, in just a few short hours, his world would be complete. Now no matter what life threw at him, he would have a safe haven to run to, a welcoming port that would help him battle any storm.

Gunter groaned.

Jerry reached his foot to the dog's back, gently caressing his fur. "Hey, old man, it's my last night as a single man. Either cut me some slack or stay out of my head."

Gunter lifted his head and gave a slight wag of his tail.

A moment later, Wayne came into view. "Is this a private party or can I join you?"

Jerry nodded toward an empty chair. "How'd you find me?"

"Lucky guess. Something told me you were awake. I remember reading a couple of the letters you sent home when you were heading overseas and recalled how you said you liked sitting under the stars."

Jerry started to tease him about using the gift, but they both knew Wayne wasn't psychic, and he didn't want to do anything to rattle the man. "Can't sleep," Jerry said instead.

"Nope," his father said as he settled into the chair. "Don't tell your ma, but I think I had too much ice cream."

Gunter groaned once more at the mention of the

tasty treat. Jerry wasn't sure if the dog was agreeing with his father or calling Wayne a lightweight. "I think Gunter has matched you bite for bite in that department."

"At least he doesn't have to worry about his waistline." Wayne sighed a heavy sigh. "What's on your mind, son?"

"What do you mean?"

"It's 2 a.m. and you're awake. I figured you had something on your mind."

"I took a walk and ended up here." Jerry shrugged. "Guess I've just been sitting here thinking of everything: past, present and future."

"Are you scared?"

Gunter lifted his head as if waiting for the answer.

"Of getting married, no," Jerry said honestly. "Of living up to expectations, maybe."

"Son, I've heard April talking to your mother. I can assure you that you've already done that. With that said, your goal shouldn't be to live up to her expectations, it should be to surpass them." Wayne grew quiet. "That little girl of yours is lucky to have you. I know I wasn't much of a father to you growing up."

"Dad."

"No, don't try to stop me. We both know it's true. I'm not going to rehash things that can't be changed. I just want you to know that I will never treat Max or any other children you might have the way I treated you. Max might not be of our blood, but I'm proud to call her my granddaughter, and she's welcome in my home anytime, with or without you."

"You've come a long way, Dad."

"Thanks, son." Wayne heaved himself from his chair. "I think I'll mosey back to my room."

Jerry smiled and nodded to Gunter. "How about you mosey back with Dad to make sure he makes it back to his room?"

Wayne frowned. "Who are you talking to?"

Jerry gave a nod to Gunter, who had scrambled to his feet the moment his father stood. "Gunter is playing bodyguard tonight."

Wayne slapped the side of his leg as his smile disappeared. "Come on, Gunter, we'll take the long way and grab us a night cap at the bar."

Gunter smiled a K-9 smile as he moved up beside Wayne.

While his father was one to enjoy an occasional beer, Jerry knew the bar his father was speaking of was the ice cream bar. "Night, Dad."

"Night, son."

Jerry sat staring at the stars for several more moments before deciding he was too cranked to sit still. He stood and bent at the waist, stretching out his back, then pulled his back leg up to stretch his calves. Once he'd repeated this process several times, he took off in a steady jog. He ran around the ship twice then proceeded up the stairs, making his way to the helo pad and circling it twice before heading back down the stairs and running the circumference of the ship a final time. When he'd finished, he made his way back to the pool deck then stripped his shirt and dove into the pool. He came up pushing the water out of his eyes with his fingers just as Gunter joined him in the pool.

***

It was nearly four in the morning before Jerry made his way back to his room and nearly 10 a.m. before he dragged himself out of bed. Though he'd not had a bachelor party, he felt very much as if he'd tied one on the night before. Sitting on the side of the bed, he moved his neck back and forth to release the kinks. Gunter was lying on April's side of the bed with his head resting on the pillow. The dog opened one eye but didn't bother to get up even when Jerry pulled the sheets up in a half-hearted attempt at making the bed.

A doorbell rang. Seconds later, his grandmother appeared in the room. "What's with the dog?"

"Me first," Jerry replied. "What's with the doorbell? Is Max okay?"

"Max is fine. If she wasn't, I wouldn't have bothered with the doorbell. I just wanted to make sure you were decent." Granny walked to the bed and poked Gunter.

The dog didn't move.

"I'm pretty sure he's in a sugar coma. He and Dad have been hitting the ice cream bar pretty much nonstop. What about you? You've been scarce of late."

"Bunny and I have been spending time at the casino."

Jerry raised an eyebrow. "Did you win anything?"

"Not us directly, but we've had fun helping others win. Oh, don't give me that look, you know those machines are rigged." Her face turned serious. "Are you excited about the big day?"

"More than you know."

"I was worried about you for a while, but you now have others to keep you company." Granny held up a hand when he started to speak. "It's okay. I'm thrilled you're building a life with family and friends. You gave me cause for concern, but now I can see you're going to be alright."

Jerry rubbed at the back of his neck. "Why does this feel like goodbye?"

"Jerry Carter McNeal, you of all people should know there is never a true goodbye. I'll be around and always when you need me. Better answer that." She nodded toward the door and faded from view.

Jerry opened the door to find Fred standing there. Dressed in a dark suit, he'd just extended his hand toward the door. Fred lowered his hand and raised the garment bag he was holding.

"What's that?" Jerry asked when Fred stepped inside and hung the bag on a hook.

Fred looked him up and down. "I know we're on a cruise ship, but I thought you might like to dress up a bit for the big event."

While he'd planned on wearing his khakis, he'd not seen April's dress. That she'd refused to show it to him let him know it was something special.

“Thanks.”

“You have the rings?”

“I do.”

“Save that for the nuptials,” Fred said and laughed at his own joke. “Do you need anything else? Say the word and I’ll make it happen.”

“Nope, this covers all bases.” Jerry held up the bag. “Thank you. Carrie, the suit… everything.”

“It’s what I do,” Fred replied. “Speaking of what I do.”

“Yes?”

“That thing you asked me to look into with Max’s biological father, it’s done.”

A deep sense of both relief and excitement surged through Jerry. “How? I didn’t doubt you could do it, but I didn’t expect it this soon.”

Fred smiled a sly smile. “We made the guy an offer he couldn’t refuse.”

While he wanted it done, Jerry didn’t like the idea of paying the man for neglecting Max. “You paid him off?”

“Do I look like the kind of person that rewards people for bad behavior? No,” Fred said, answering his own question. “My attorney had a word with the man and explained the situation. He also let him know if he decided not to sign the papers that April would be filing an immediate claim for back child support, and given that Max is going on fourteen, the man saw the value of making the right decision.”

Jerry was immediately incensed. Max was a terrific kid and one he’d give his life to protect.

Anger fueled his veins. "You mean he sold her out?!"

Feeling his anger, Gunter growled a menacing growl and moved to his side, leaning into him and offering emotional support.

Oblivious to the dog's presence, Fred pulled himself taller. "Don't shoot the messenger. And before you go puffing up on me, keep your eye on the big picture."

Fred was right. After he and April were married, he would be able to legally adopt Max. "The papers are signed?"

Fred reached into his jacket pocket, withdrew an envelope and handed it to him. "Signed, sealed and delivered. Consider it a wedding present."

Jerry gripped the envelope, surprising himself at how intense the moment was. Fred must have known, as he reached a hand to his shoulder. "You're a good man, McNeal. April and Max are just as lucky to have you as you are to have them."

Not trusting himself to answer without emotion, Jerry merely nodded.

***

Jerry stood on the upper deck of the helo port, which had been transformed into a magical wedding venue. Instead of the marked landing zone, the area now boasted artificial grass, a white canopy and an arched arbor decorated with green vines and small white flowers. A small group of chairs sat facing the arch, and instead of being cordoned off in two sections, the chairs were centered and filled with their small group of family and friends. Instead of running down the middle, a bright white runner trailed off to the side.

Gunter stood sentinel on the runner, ears twitching. The dog lifted his head and sniffed the air, then lowered his nose and followed the runner. Jerry resisted the urge to follow the dog. *Easy, McNeal, you've come this far. Trust the process.*

The captain moved into position as the music started and everyone, Jerry included, looked to the side as Max and Houdini made their way onto the runner. Dressed in a pale pink dress, Max's hair was pulled high on her head with the sides flowing around her face in soft wisps, making her look much older than her thirteen years. Jerry made a mental note to get with Fred to rev up Max's self-defense training. Gunter appeared at Jerry's side, looking at him as if to say, *Don't worry, Jer, me and the boy won't let anything happen to her.*

He felt her presence and then April was there.

While he knew she would look beautiful, he was not prepared to see her wearing a white satin wedding dress that barely hugged her curves. With her hair piled on her head and lips painted ruby red, she looked very much like a glamorous movie star from the golden era. He briefly wondered if Fred had a hand in what she was wearing but knew he had not. He had so many questions. How had she known he would ask her to marry him while on the cruise? Why hadn't she warned him he'd need something more than khakis? And mostly, how on earth did he get so lucky? He'd ask those questions later, when there weren't so many eyes and ears. Instead, he mouthed a single word.

WOW!

Fred nodded his agreement.

A lovely pink blush crept up her cheeks as Fred stopped, gave her a kiss on the cheek and whispered something in her ear. Taking the last few steps alone, April stopped in front of him.

The captain waited for Fred to take his seat then began. "Dearly beloved, we are gathered here aboard this vessel on the open sea to witness the joining of Jerry Carter McNeal and April Renee Buchanan in marriage. I understand they have written their own vows. If you would like to begin." He gave a nod to Jerry.

Jerry took April's hands and met her gaze. "I have traveled the world always looking for something I couldn't seem to find and running from things I couldn't control, and through it all, I've felt unsettled. Today, as we begin our life together as husband and wife, I have no reservations, and I no longer fear the future. With you by my side, I know I can handle anything. I promise to love you, and honor you and keep you safe."

April smiled a trembling smile. "I wasn't looking for anyone when you came into my life, but now that you're here, I can't imagine my life without you. You've shown me what it feels like to be treated with love and respect and have given me a chance at a future I never dreamed possible."

The captain turned to Jerry. "Do you have the rings?"

Max came forward with Houdini. Jerry stooped and removed both ring cases from the pouch on the shepherd's harness. He peeked inside each box and handed one to April.

"These rings are a symbol of your voyage together. An unbroken circle of your love and commitment. You may place the rings." He stepped back and waited as they each slipped a ring on the other's hand.

"By the power vested in me as the captain of this ship, and according to maritime tradition and law, I now pronounce you husband and wife. You may kiss the bride."

As Jerry pulled April into his arms, a roar went up as not only those on the helo pad, but hundreds of onlookers filled the air with cheers.

The captain patted the air with his hands. "If we could have your attention for one more moment." He looked at Jerry.

Jerry turned and motioned Max forward. Kneeling on one knee, he pulled a box from his pocket and opened it to show a pair of diamond stud earrings. "Maxine Renee Buchanan, would you do me the honor of being my daughter?"

Max frowned. "I thought if you married my mom, I would be your daughter."

"You are, and you always will be, but I would like to give you my name as well."

Tears welled in Max's eyes. "You mean I will be

a McNeal like you and Mom?"

"Yes."

Max bobbed her head. "Oh, Jerry!" Max draped her arms around Jerry's neck as once again those watching cheered their approval.

***

Jerry entered the stateroom aiming to retrieve April's wrap. Upon entering the room, he saw a bottle of champagne in a bucket of ice, along with a small plate of chocolate-covered strawberries. He smiled. "Good ole Fred."

As he lifted the note, he knew the gift wasn't from Fred.

Jerry, I thought we were friends, and yet, I don't recall getting an invitation to your wedding. Just to show you there are no ill feelings, here is a small gift for you and your bride. Don't worry, it's not business, just personal.

Your connection to the other side on this side,
Mario Fabel

Jerry stared at the note in awe. While he knew Mario had connections, the fact he'd gotten wind of their nuptials was beyond comprehension. Not for the first time, Jerry was glad the mobster considered him a friend instead of a foe.

The End

A note from the author

As many of you already know, I am dealing with the aftereffects of having Bell's Palsy.

While I have made great strides in my recovery, I continue to have some lingering issues that do not react well to stress. For that reason, while I will continue to write, I will no longer place my books on preorder until they are nearly finished. My new plan is to work on multiple manuscripts at once until one of them takes the lead.

To stay updated with future releases and preorders, I kindly request that you take two steps: first, visit my website and sign up for my newsletter. Second, follow me on Amazon, as they will send you an email to tell you about new releases and pre-orders.

Thank you for reading. I promise to give you something new very soon!

~ Sherry A. Burton

Check out **www.sherryaburton.com** to sign up
for my newsletter and order autographed
copies, audiobooks, shirts, cups and more.

About the Author

Sherry A. Burton writes in multiple genres and has won numerous awards for her books. Sherry's awards include the coveted Charles Loring Brace Award, for historical accuracy within her historical fiction series, The Orphan Train Saga. Sherry is a member of the National Orphan Train Society, presents lectures on the history of the orphan trains, and is listed on the NOTC Speaker's Bureau as an approved speaker.

Originally from Kentucky, Sherry and her Retired Navy Husband now call Michigan home. Sherry enjoys traveling and spending time with her husband of more than forty-four years.